D1048632

JUJU

Life on the East Side

TAMARIO PETTIGREW

Copyright © 2019 by Tamario Pettigrew
All rights reserved. This book or any portion thereof may not be reproduced or used in any manner whatsoever without the express written permission of the publisher except for the use of brief quotations in a book review.

Publisher's note: This is a work of fiction. Names, characters, places, and incidents either are the product of the author's imagination or are used fictitiously. Any resemblance to actual events, locales, or persons, living or dead, is entirely coincidental.

Edited by Kristen Corrects, Inc.
Book Cover Design by ebooklaunch.com
First edition published 2019

1

We moved back to the worst part of the ghetto over the summer. On our drive back, I was in the front seat between my oldest brother Morris and my mother's boyfriend. Morris was in his element, leaning out the passenger window, shouting to his friends. People in the worst part of the ghetto respect Morris because he went to prison. Also, because he's a good fighter. Once he beat this chump they said was going for Golden Gloves. This chump was a light heavyweight. He was bigger than Morris. Taller. With longer arms. It didn't matter. Morris knocked him right on his back. He was out. Since then, a lot of people been afraid of Morris. I see them refusing his eye contact. Don't nobody ever bother him. Plus, Morris knows everybody. He got one of them popular personalities where he always happy to see you, even if he just saw you two minutes ago. People like him. He makes them feel important. Sometimes, I imagine if we wasn't born in the ghetto, he'd be a politician or somethin'. Mama thought he was gon' be a boxer, but he ain't never have the dedication.

The deeper our U-Haul got into the worse part of the ghetto, the more I sweated. My stomach was rumbling—nerves. It was the sight of all these poor people that made me nervous. It made me anxious. It made my heart slow. It made me wish things could be different. I try not to focus on stuff like sadness and poverty but sometimes my heart makes me.

Morris said that was my "big problem." He said, "You too smart for your own good. Nobody thinks about shit like you. What's wrong with you? Think about how Mama gon' always give us her last piece of bread, even if she ain't ate in days. Put yo mind on that. All these books ain't gon' get you nothin'. They'a have yo ass smart and hungry. Fuck that. Get money."

I tried to listen to Morris most times, but my mind ain't like his. I can't only think about thriving in the ghetto and surviving day to day and how I'm gon' eat and what clothes I got and what makes me better than other black boys. It ain't the way I am. I think about staying who I am and not letting the ghetto become part of my mind. I tell myself I can make it out. I just can't let it get to me.

All I think about is escaping the ghetto. Morris told me one time. "You can't help people the way you want to cuz if you do, they get better, and you get worse. Everything has a cost. You know like that smart motha fucka say, 'For every action there is an equal and opposite reaction.' What's his name? You know who I'm talkin' 'bout."

I thought it was only Morris who thought like that, because of how he went to prison, but it ain't. A lot of people in the ghetto is just like Morris. They don't think about making it out of the ghetto. They think about ruling the ghetto, and being celebrated in the ghetto.

I watched poor people carry their groceries from corner stores. I watched men drink beer from paper bag-covered cans. I watched boys not much older than me gambling in a dice game right out in the open. I watched a boy my age stalking a black lady. He was creepin' and sneakin' and plannin'. I wanted to warn her, but before I could, he snatched her purse and kept running. It was a lady older than Mama. Morris was hyped over it.

"Yo, you seen that? He got that shit. Get yo money. Get yo money and keep getting up. That's what I'm talking 'bout."

I was watching the old lady. She was on her back in the street, oblivious to that stalking of her purse she just went through. I was sad for her. It wasn't his money. That money he stole belonged to her. Morris was clappin' and laughing to himself. I kept watchin', wishin' I could help her. Hoping she wasn't hurt. I watched so long, my head turned until she was out of sight. I tried to watch from the side view mirror but we was too far away to see anything but little dots in the mirror.

We kept going deeper into the ghetto. Morris was halfway out the window saying, "Hey, my man," and "Aye, baby. What's up?" One time at the red light he called to this girl he knew. "Ta'Sheka? Ta'Sheka?"

She was fine—thick in all the right places. She had one of them booties only girls in the ghetto have. She was pretty. At first, she turned with a mean face, which grew into a wide grin. A lot of people in the ghetto have mean faces. They ain't really mean, though. They're just protecting themselves from the life you have to live when you're born in the ghetto.

"I'ma call you!" Morris shouted.

She threw her hand like he was lying.

When he wasn't shouting out the window, he was playing with the radio, and singing in my ear. When I didn't laugh at his singing, Morris' face looked concerned.

"What's wrong?" Morris said.

"Nothin'."

Morris was looking at me like he was my father. I was hoping he ain't hear my heart thinking about that old lady who got her purse snatched. I was hoping he didn't or he'd start talking about the need to toughen me up, for my own good. "Don't nobody care," he always telling me. "People don't give a fuck. You was born alone and you gon' die alone." He was always tough like that. He was concerned though, I could tell.

He said, "You gon' be alright. All's you gotta do is get one person to know yo name, and that's how you get a lot of friends."

The buildings got worse, more dilapidated. I was looking at Morris and he was cool as a cucumber. He ain't have no sweat on him. It felt like Morris was happy. When we left our old house, it seemed like everybody was happy, even though I know they wasn't. It was like they wasn't even thinking about how bad it could get down here.

That's all I thought about, how bad it was gon' be.

I knew returning wasn't gon' go good for me. I knew there was things I was gon' have to do if I wanted to fit in. I wasn't worried about making friends. I was worried about making it out the ghetto. I was worried about what kind of boy I'd have to be to survive.

I was just nervous the streets would consume me, and I'd never be me again.

2

When we parked, we were in front of a shack. The East Side of Buffalo, NY, is a segregated slum. If you've ever been here, you know I'm telling the truth. If you ever been here, you'd know it's filthy, and overgrown, and dilapidated, and uncared for. You'd know that it's rude and loud and busy. You'd know that fights and laughter and music spring from every corner. If you ever been here, you'd know it smells of a heavy dankness, coming off all them manufacturing plants, in the summer. You'd know the old broken-down houses smell like mold, stale air, lead paint, and plaster cover-ups. One time a house Mama rented smelled like smoke. We figured the house was in a fire before we moved in. The white man renting it just covered the burned wood with a coat of paint. He wouldn't even let Mama out of her lease.

The only nice things on the East Side is all the big churches. I mean they nice to look at. Sometimes if Mama drive by one of them big stone churches on Broadway Avenue, I be wondering who built them. I be looking at them, stone by stone, like someone put together a giant puzzle. Wondering if God told man to build them nice churches—or if man built them, so he could say he has a bigger and better God than people who don't have big churches. Mama said it don't matter, she said, "Church is in your heart." She said, "If you believe in God, he will believe in you."

I don't believe in nothin' no more. Not even God.

When we parked in front of the new place, Mama came around to the passenger door with a bright smile like she just bought this shack we're moving into.

"This it."

Her boyfriend Elijah, who looked old enough to be my grandfather, told Mama how nice the place was, and so did Morris.

"JuJu?" Mama smiled expectantly.

I didn't like it. I didn't want to move down here.

Mama nodded. "Check it out."

Before I could check it out, my three younger sisters ran past me in a blur of colorful hair baubles and barrettes holding their twisted hair together, claiming bedrooms.

It was alright. It was a house. You know, normal ghetto stuff. Uncut grass. Failing roof shingles. Peeling paint. Inside was dingy and worn and broken-down. Filled with bad cover-ups. The steps to the second floor felt like they was one wrong move from falling in. Every step I took squealed like a pig. The toilet took three passes before Mama got it white. The kitchen was missing some of them fake asbestos floor tiles. The cabinet doors wouldn't close like they was supposed to. The faucet had a drip. The sink had a black spot where it caught the drip from the faucet. When I flicked on the kitchen lights to see if they worked, it took a second before any light was given. When we plugged in our refrigerator, the lights blinked.

Elijah, who's always in his blue mechanics uniform, said, "Probably got a shortage."

Mama was just smiling at me with her Jheri curl shining. She was wearing leather sandals, white jeans, and this beige-mustard colored T-shirt she got from the check cashing place on the West Side, which said *Spicy* on the front. There was a big red chili pepper with a goofy Mexican smile right in the middle of it. Mama liked it. She had one of them on again, off again personalities. When she was on, she was goofy like a little girl. When she was off, she was mean. One time she ain't talk to Morris for months because the cops came to the house looking for him.

Mama looked at me. "At least we got a roof over our head."

It was better than my cousin Keith who got homeless one winter and had to live in the city mission with his mother and little sister. I asked Mama if they could stay with us, but she said I better be thankful I got somewhere to stay. Ain't nobody take them in. All the women kept saying his mother was "nasty." My other cousin Spoon was homeless one time too after his mother lost her jobs in the recession.

A lot of people get homeless in the ghetto. I hear people asking Mama if they can sleep on her couch. Mama always telling them, "I got seven kids." Every now and again, someone will sleep on our couch, but Mama don't like it. One time when Mama's friend Pooch slept on our couch, Mama locked my sisters in their bedroom, so they couldn't get out and he couldn't get in. She did that when she went to work on her night job. "Don't let nothing happen to yo sisters, you hear me?" she whispered to me before she left. "I'm going'na work. I'a be back soon as I get off. Anything happen, call the police. You hear me?"

"Yeah, Mama."

From time to time, I'd used the bathroom even though I ain't have to. Just so I could see if Pooch was asleep on the couch. One time I was just standing there looking at him, trying to see if he was sleep. He opened his eyes. "What the fuck you looking at?" I ain't say nothin'. I went to bed. He ain't never try nothing with my sisters. After a couple of days, he found somewhere else to sleep.

I found my bedroom at the top of the steps. It was a dark-paneled hole at the front of the house with two windows to the street. There was some low angles in the ceiling so the room felt smaller when I stood in some spots. There was this heavy smell of chalk and dust throughout the second floor but especially in my room. I stood thinking my bed would go against the wall, away from the windows. There wasn't no closet and I ain't have no real dresser. The one I had in the working-class house was built into the wall and wasn't one that Mama purchased for me. I didn't want to complain. Mama always had a tough time finding houses big enough for us and this was the first single-family house we moved into since we lived down here several years ago. We'd always end up in apartments and sometimes I'd have to sleep on the couch because there wasn't enough bedrooms. Here I could get away. I could close my door. It just felt right. Felt like I was home when I was in my room with the door closed.

Outside was a different story. Outside was the ghetto.

When I went out on the porch thinking I would help move our stuff in, Morris walked past me with Mama's queen-size mattress. "I got it," he said.

Through the roar of traffic, yapping horns, noisy engines, and exhaust backfires, I heard a voice full of laughter say, "Bump you." When I looked, it was a boy about my age laughing in the bright sun three doors down. He had the biggest smile I'd ever seen on a kid from the ghetto. I later learned his name was Ashley. Five boys stood below his stoop looking up at him like he was some exalted leader of men. He had a low brush cut so you could see waves in his hair. He wore these thick dirty winter jeans, though it was nearly ninety degrees, and a dingy Yankees baseball jacket, the white one with blue pinstripes. His sneakers seemed too big for him, like they was passed down. The fake gold necklace he wore seemed thin and tarnished like he got it out of one of them candy machines.

Elijah woke me from their laughter. "Stay here till we come back with the rest of y'all stuff." He was poking his old finger right in my chest.

"I'm coming," I said.

Morris agreed with Elijah. "Somebody gotta stay till we get back. You'a be alright."

Morris always said that to me. If Mama told him to stay with me and my sisters while she went to work at her night job, he'd smack my shoulder and say, "You'a be alright" as he disappeared into the night.

I wasn't paying attention. I was watching this big dude Morris knew walking past our porch. "Y'all over here now, huh?" he said.

Morris said, "Yeah, we back."

Even he was afraid to look Morris in the eye. He kept walking.

Morris said, "I'll be around." Morris had that effect on everybody, he was a real tough guy.

I was thinking this big dude Morris knew was coming to scope out our electronics. We have a lot of electronics from Okinawa, because my second oldest brother Terrence is in the Air Force. I even got a Walkman from Japan, for my Christmas gift. Terrence is smarter than the rest of us because he left Buffalo soon as he finished high school. One time, after he got into a big fight in high school, he was real miserable over it. I could tell he ain't like hitting people. He just couldn't get over it. He said, "This not how life supposed to be." He was convinced people in the ghetto only befriend you so they can start trouble. After high school, he joined the military. One time when Mama ain't move us and he'd sent half his pay, I heard him say, "The only way y'all gon' change is to leave Buffalo. Y'all must like it there. It's like a prison, Mama. It ain't like that in the rest of the world. Y'all need to get outta there and see what life is really like." He was on the phone with Mama from Germany. He was always saying, "Buffalo ain't normal. The ghetto like a concentration camp." He said, "It's violent." He was telling me that when I got on the phone with him.

"You bet not drop outta high school."

"I'm only in the eighth grade."

"So what? Don't be in the streets. Them boys in the streets be trying to make you believe things that ain't true. Think for yo'self. Don't be out there fightin'."

He told me all about what happened when he was in England, on the train. When the train made a stop, "It picked up all these black people in good work clothes and these white jackets." All these black people, he said, were doctors and lawyers and pharmacists. He said he ain't never seen nothing like that in the States. He was telling me I could be something like that because I was smart. That was right before we moved. "Stay out the streets. It's dangerous out there."

Sometimes, I listen to Terrence. Sometimes I don't. I mean, he ain't my father or nothin'. It's tough to know who to listen to. Morris is the oldest, so sometimes I have to listen to him. They—Morris and Terrence—was as different as night and day, though. Morris built a reputation off fighting. He'a fight for anything. He'a fight for nothing. It's just the way he is. It ain't like his fighting has to be just, either. In the ghetto, boys like Morris are always ready to fight you over nothin'. They'a start a fight with you because you too dark, or too light, or too tall, or too short. They always tryin'na fight you, so people will know they'a fight anybody, anytime, anywhere.

When I was watching that hulk walk away, Morris slapped my shoulder.

"You'a be alright. We comin' right back."

Morris had just started his reconditioning toward freedom a couple months before we had to return to the worst part of the ghetto. The state had him in a work release program for a while. He finished it. He had a parole officer, but he basically free now.

Elijah gave me the key to the place. "I locked the back door. Stay out here on the porch."

I looked at Mama. Mama said, "We comin' right back."

They left me standing on our new porch. I stood there watching our neighbors circle to feel me out. That's how it works in the ghetto. If you have anything worth stealing, you have'ta watch it day and night, or someone will take it. Usually, people move in to a new place under cover of darkness. If it wasn't for Elijah's wife, we woulda moved in past midnight. Elijah was the only one who could drive the truck.

I was alone on our new porch. I was watching them, and they was watching me. I could feel it. Even the old lady next door was peeping at me through her curtains. Every time someone passed, I'd cross or uncross my arms. Or take my hands out of my pockets. Or frown. In the ghetto, you learn expressive ways of speaking without saying anything. I was trying to let them know I wasn't scared. That I was tough. Most of the real tough guys never argue, they just use their face to convey the message. Even if you was scared, you had to pretend like you wasn't. In the ghetto, being scared gets you victimized. You have to act like you ain't scared of nothin'.

When I came back from the bathroom, Ashley passed me twice. Once he passed making a whistle as he ignored me, all bravado. I had my arms crossed but he didn't look my way. On his way back, he sucked a blue huggie he got from Webbers. As he approached, he nodded. I nodded a return but neither of us said anything. He was feeling me out.

That's how it works in the ghetto. They want you to know they control the streets. Especially if you new.

He wanted me to understand he was the leader here. This happens all the time in the ghetto. Dudes be tryin' to gain a reputation. Sometimes the best way to gain a rep is to hit the biggest dude first. On the first day you move on a new street, you're supposed to walk up to the biggest, toughest dude on the block, and knock him out. Just hit him. Swing for the fences. Throw a haymaker. Even if he kicks your ass, at worst, you're the number two. It's one of the rules around here. *Never let them outrank you. Never settle for the bottom.* Plus, they'll think you don't mind a fight. Because of it, they'll usually leave you alone. Or, they'll become your flunky. Your lackey. Your yes-man. If you do end up on the bottom, you'll never stop fighting. Even punks will try to fight you if you're on the bottom.

I knew I should return Ashley's nod because that was part of the challenge. You can't show no nerves. You have to be brave. You have to stare them right in they eye and let them know you ain't no punk.

That's what I did with Ashley. I didn't make any missteps. I ain't back down one inch. I watched him as he walked to his stoop. I saw him stub his toe and try to act like it didn't happen.

He sat on the top step with his boys, looking up at him. In his crew was Kevin, who is also taller than me, though Ashley is the tallest. Kevin's got the build of an inside linebacker. He said he weighed 230 pounds. There's Chill, who was nearly Kevin's equal. Chill has a belly and some fat around his temples, though. There were twin brothers Ronald and Donald, who we called Ronron and Dondon. Like me, Ronron and Dondon are exactly six feet tall. I'm tall and skinny like my father, who people sometimes say is my twin. Lastly, there's Marquis, Ashley's little brother. He ain't nine yet, though he told everyone he was ten. Like most black boys, he was big for his age.

After we got our things moved in, I came and sat on the steps near midnight. I was hot and tired from helping my sisters set up their beds. Ashley and Kevin was still down there talking. I was thinking about going to introduce myself. On Humboldt Parkway, I learned you have to walk up to someone and say, "Hi, I'm JuJu. What's your name?" They probably woulda laughed at me if I did that. They probably woulda thought I was a sucka.

Mama came back with a pizza from Bocce's, so I didn't.

3

In the morning, I woke up late. When we lived on Humboldt Parkway, I woke early because every car would start at the same time. Everyone was going to work. I didn't hear any of that this morning.

I wished we didn't have to move. I missed Humboldt Parkway. I missed all the people like Mr. Williams, who paid me to cut his grass, and Mrs. Addison, who was married to a mean black man who called the cops on me. He said I threw a bottle at his car. I didn't. I needed the bottle to prop open my bedroom window, and when I was trying to put it in one day, it fell and hit his car. He was always angry, talking about, "Don't walk on my grass," "Don't touch my gate," "Don't stand by my car." There are a lot of old timers like him in the ghetto, mad for a reason that ain't got nothin' to do with you. Mad cuz they got old. Mad cuz they ain't make it out the ghetto. Mad cuz life don't never change in the ghetto.

Mama said, "Stay away from him. He crazy. He think he better than us, that's his problem."

There was another lady across the street, Mrs. Shumaker, who was a teacher. She had two daughters who used to play with my sisters. In the summer when Mama was working two jobs, Mrs. Shumaker would take us to Delaware Park. She was younger than Mama and they was always talking about how black men ain't "no good, no more." Mrs. Shumaker's husband left her the same way my father left Mama. For a younger woman.

Sometimes we'd go to her house if Mama was working her third job as a nanny on weekends. She kept saying she loved kids but I think she wanted us around because her husband was gone. Sometimes when my sisters played with her daughters, she would make me help her cook. She would always yell, "JuJu, come help me." She was always talking to me like I was normal, asking me what I liked, what I wanted to eat, if I had a girlfriend and stuff like that. She ain't never treat me different.

One time she was making mashed potatoes, fried chicken, and canned corn. She said, "This ain't right without some wine." She smiled. She drank a sip she already poured, hidden on the side of her coffee machine. With a wink, she put her finger over her lips saying not to tell my sisters or her daughters, who were playing in her daughter's bedroom. She put her wine glass down and said, "Now, about these potatoes." She already cut them and put them in a pot. I helped. They was boiling and bubbling and making all kinds of white scum on top of the water.

"You ever mashed a potato?" she asked.

"No."

"Here, let me show you." She took another sip of wine. "Take this. Then you get this." She showed me how to drain the water into a colander. "Now take this." She got the masher and poked me in the belly with it. She was smiling a little girl smile I hadn't seen before. "Take it." I thought she was gon' poke me again. She didn't. She handed the potato masher over to me. When I was mashing, she put her hand around mine and said, "You gotta mash it harder than that." She was all warm standing behind me mashing them potatoes. "Mash it hard, you ain't gon' hurt it." She had her other hand on my hip. "There, like that. Stir it around. Mash it."

"Like this?"

She smacked me on the butt and said, "Like that. Good. Keep mashing."

When we was eating, she was telling how "JuJu made the potatoes." My sisters didn't believe her, and she winked at me again.

I loved going over her house. She was always telling me I was gon' be a good boyfriend and a good husband and a good father. "Because I can tell," she said. "You'll make some woman happy. You're going to be a good man, JuJu." Most people in the ghetto tell you, "You ain't gon' be shit, and you dumb, and black, and no good." Mrs. Shumaker wasn't like that. She was telling me I was a good kid and I was gon' live a good life.

There was this other lady, Khoral, who almost made the United States Olympics gymnastics team. She would run and flip the entire street, from stop sign to stop sign. She had a son named Roman who could walk on his hands the same as I walk on my feet. Sometimes he'd walk up a flight of stairs on his palms. He could even run a race on his hands. He was in high school, so he ain't hardly play with us, unless his mother was out flipping and doing gymnastics. Sometimes, he'd let me come and play Atari with him. Mama would get mad if I wasn't home with my sisters and she'd come down after she got off work.

"Didn't I tell you to stay with yo sister?"

"I was playing the game."

"Fuck that game. Anything liable to happen."

Mama was always saying that because the year before we got the second-floor apartment on Humboldt Parkway, a man tried to kidnap my baby sisters. The police never found out who he was. Mama said that was my job. To look out for them. To die for them. I would, too. I would sacrifice my entire life for them, if I had to.

Mama was especially vocal of me watching over my sisters now that we had to move back to the worst part of the ghetto. I didn't have to watch over them as much on Humboldt Parkway. Them women watched over the kids there.

When we first moved over there, I punched this boy named Richard in the face. He was walking around with his head in the clouds. He had all the new toys. Spoiled. He got whatever he wanted. He had every Transformer. He had all of the Coleco arcade games. He had *Donkey Kong*, *Frogger*, *Pac Man*, and *Galaxian*. He had Atari and this shiny new bike.

I heard him yelling at his mother because his bike broke. He was calling her names under his breath because she told him, "Your father will fix it when he gets home." When I crossed the street to look at his bike, he said, "Don't touch it."

"I was gon' fix it."

I fixed a lot of bikes for my sisters. Mama was always buying us broken bikes white kids don't want no more from the flea market up on Walden Avenue. He got between me and his bike.

"Get your own bike."

He was standing there like he was tough. I bet he ain't never even been hungry before. I been hungry plenty of times. I ain't have nothing but a boiled egg and a bowl of oatmeal for breakfast, every day. For lunch I ain't have nothin' but an old carrot, and some crackers and peanut butter Mama got from the government. Most of the time we ain't even have nothing for dinner but a piece of that government cheese. If we was lucky Mama bought some bread and we got to have grilled cheese for dinner. If we wasn't lucky Mama would tell us to go to bed. She'd tell us to "sleep it off." Sleep ain't never help. Most times, I'd spend all night rocking and tossing and turning, and Mama would get mad at me if I was still hungry and came to drink a lot of water. Whenever I drank a lot of water for dinner, I'd pee the bed and Mama would get mad because we ain't have no washing machine and she'd have to carry a bag of pissy sheets to the Laundromat.

Richard was just standing there trying to look tough. He kept crossing his arms and looking at me real hard.

So, I hit him. I hit him good too. He went crying to his mother.

All them women on Humboldt Parkway came telling me, "It's not right to hit." They was telling me how blacks have to get along because "We all we got."

The next day I was at Mrs. Shumaker's house with my sisters. Mama paid her twenty dollars to watch us while she worked as a nanny over the weekend.

"You have to be careful, because you're so tall," Mrs. Shumaker was telling me. "You can't go off hitting people. It's not nice. What'd you hit him for?"

"I don't know."

She took a breath and said, "God I'll tell ya, even black men hate black men."

I didn't hate him. I just hit him. It wasn't a big deal.

I don't know, maybe she was right. Maybe I hated that he was richer than me. He had everything you could want and still seemed ungrateful.

Mrs. Shumaker left me alone. I was just sitting on her stringy couch, thinking about it. She came back with a notebook.

"When I was in college, I learned if I write about it, I can get it off my chest," she said. "You don't have to, but it worked for me."

I took the notebook.

4

I tried to talk Mama out of moving, but she said, "We don't have no choice." She said, "Because I can't afford it, gotdamnit."

I missed Humboldt Parkway. I felt like the people understood me on Humboldt Parkway.

Truthfully, I didn't want to leave Jenifer. She was the first girl I ever liked, the first girl I ever kissed.

It happened right before Mama said we was moving. We was playing hide-and-go-get-it. We had to hurry. Jenifer had to be home before the streetlights came on. I knew where she hid. Every time we played, Jenifer hid in this utility room attached to the back of her house. After the boys counted and the girls hid, I went straight to the utility room and opened the door. Jenifer was standing in the darkness. When I flipped the switch, her smile was lit by a noisy light over the door. I went in and kissed her.

I didn't want to move, to leave Jenifer. It was just something about her. Most people I meet in the ghetto don't have what she has. She's pretty, but what I like most is she don't have no ghetto face. She ain't never frowning. She has the easiest smile. It's like God made her pleasant to look at and pleasant to be around. Whenever I saw her chocolate face through her screen door, the hair on the back of my neck stood up. My heart would skip. I would smile for no reason.

When it was clear we was moving, Jenifer tied this braided bracelet on my wrist. She braided it herself. She said, "It's a boondoggle."

When we first met, she was friends with my sister Boo. Boo knew I liked her so if her father was being mean Boo would come and sit on her porch. Her father would let Boo come in their house, but not me. After a while her father didn't hate me. He didn't even try to keep me away from her. To him I was just Boo's brother.

Easter 1986 was one of the hottest Easters in Buffalo's history. It was almost eighty degrees. 1986 was hot in general and people in the ghetto kept saying Earth was returning to Hell in June. Apparently, June 6 would mark three sixes on the calendar and most black people thought that meant Earth was entering "the sign of the beast." I didn't believe it because no one would tell me why Earth didn't end June 6, 1976 or June 6, 1966. They would just say, "Because it didn't."

We were all outside playing when Jenifer's father asked me to go to the store with her so nothing happened to her or her bike. Mama said people trust me. She said I have trusting eyes. "People think you innocent, so they trust you."

I walked, and Jenifer rode this pink bike she got for her thirteenth birthday. She came out the store. "Hold this." She got on her bike. "Okay," she said. She reached for her bag. I didn't return it.

"I got it. I'll carry it."

She just smiled and shook her head when I wouldn't give it back. "What if you get hit by a car because you have to carry this?"

Her father started asking me all these questions after that. He asked what high school I was going to. I didn't have an answer. I didn't know. No one ever asked me that before. Most of the kids I knew didn't even want to go to high school. The city is always sending black boys to Kensington or South Park. I doubted I even had a choice. They just say, "Black boy, go here." Then you get there and it's a warzone. Even Morris dropped out of Kensington because it's violent.

Her father said, "Jenifer's gon' go to Hutch Tech." Hutch Tech is the second-best public school in Buffalo, behind City Honors. The Hutch Tech kids usually go on to become engineers or nurses or medical technicians, or something smart like that. Some even become doctors.

Her father started letting me and Jenifer do homework on his porch. At first, we would talk and I would watch Jenifer do her homework. Her father asked, "You ain't got no homework?" I hadn't been doing my homework since *Challenger* exploded. I ain't like school no more.

"If you ain't gon' do yo homework, I don't want you bothering Jenifer while she doin' hers."

So, I started doing my homework again.

He kept telling me to finish school. "And never let them talk you out of going to college. They're gonna all tell you no. They're gonna all tell you to join the military. Go to college." He kept telling me that, repeatedly. "College. Go to college."

I didn't even think about it. It was a lot to think about and I ain't want to think about it. I ain't wanna think that far. I was just thinking about making it to the next day or the next week or to the end of the school year. I ain't never think about nothing that far in the future. College? I didn't never think about it. I ain't even know nobody who was in college. If I did go, and I ain't saying I wanted to, but if I did, I'd be the first in my family to ever attend.

When we was moving, it was the first time Jenifer gave me a hug in front of her father. We didn't kiss, but I wanted to.

When I was saying my final goodbyes, Jenifer's father shook my hand. "Remember what I told you. College. You're a smart young man. I told yo'

Mama you's smart. Go to college no matter what they say about you down there in that jungle. Don't let them change you. You got me?"

"Yeah."

"Huh?"

"Yes. I hear you."

"Good."

When you're a kid, that's what adults do. They keep telling you about this glorious future you'll have. You gon' go to college and get married and all that happy stuff. You gon' raise some children and have a good job. You gon' buy a big house and go on vacations. It's always happy. They don't never tell you about the sadness of life. They think you're too young for sad stuff and they try to keep it from you. Even in the ghetto, adults try their best to give you a good life.

That's the thing about happiness—it's prevalent even when times are their toughest. At least that's what it's like in the ghetto. In the ghetto a man without a house will smile and tell you, "I'll have a mansion next year. Watch." They want you to believe them too. They always have some scheme that's gon' make them rich, but they never get rich. They never get no mansion. They never make it out of the ghetto.

I was trying to be happy even though I was sad about moving. I was trying to have that hope, like everything was gon' work in my favor. I was remembering all them people on Humboldt Parkway. They was like family to me. They was always looking out for us, mostly because Mama had three jobs and she'd be gone for days, working, so we could have "a better life." Mama would always get mad if we ask why she ain't been home from work. She'd say, "Look, I'm bussin' my ass tryin' to give y'all a better life." Now we back in the heart of the ghetto because Mama lost one of her jobs.

I didn't even wanna get out of bed. I was lying there thinking about Humboldt Parkway, thinking about all the faces I missed, especially Jenifer's.

I jumped out of bed determined to go over on Humboldt Parkway, to see her. I was gonna get Mama's old ten-speed and ride it over there. I went into Mama's bedroom looking for it. She was sleeping. Her bike wasn't in there. I looked out the back door, into the hall. It wasn't back there. Out on the porch, I found, Mama had it chained to the metal railings. I was dejected. I was gonna go back in her bedroom and get the key from her purse, but when I opened her door and went to her purse, she rolled over.

"Don't be going through my gotdamn purse."

I didn't even get to open it. As soon as I touched it, she woke up.

"I ain't raise you to be no thief. G'on. Get yo ass outta here. And don't be bussin' in my door no more, either. You need to learn how to knock."

"I ain't wanna wake you up."

"G'on and get yo ass outta here. I mighta been changing my gotdamn clothes. I mighta had a friend in here." She reached over and grabbed her purse. "Close my gotdamn door." She put her purse on the floor between the wall and her bed.

I closed her door.

5

I felt like an outcast. I was just staying around the house, reading *To Kill a Mockingbird* again. I was staying in my bedroom hoping I didn't have to fight. They always making you fight.

I kept busy helping Mama set up her furniture and unpacking boxes. I played board games with my sisters and watched TV when I could. For the first couple of days, I went to school and came back to my bedroom. Mama said, "Isolation ain't good for nobody."

Last night I woke up after midnight because I heard people shouting. When I looked out my window, I saw the lady across the street, Cynthia, running away from a parked car. She was arguing with her ex-husband.

"Bitch, I'a kill you," he shouted in the street. "I'a kill you and I'a kill myself."

Cynthia took off running back in the house and her ex-husband fired off some shots at her before he jumped in his car and sped off.

I was watching the stillness, thinking maybe her ex-husband killed her. Ain't nobody come to check on her or nothin'. Maybe she dead. Maybe one of his bullets came through the door and killed her.

My heart was racing. Something had to be done. I was gonna go check on her.

When I got to the front room Mama was kneeling on her good couch, watching through a crack she made in the curtain with her fingers.

"What you doin' up this late?" she asked me.

"You think she dead?"

"What?"

"The lady across the street, you think she dead?"

"Go to sleep, boy."

I didn't go to sleep. I couldn't. I wanted to know if she was dead. I wanted to see if she ain't have no more blood in her and her body looked like somebody left an apple to wither. It wouldn'tna been the first time I seen a dead person.

The first dead man I saw was Bird. He was a real cool dude. He'd always let me ride his bike when he was in the house planning a crime with my brothers. He'd even give me a dollar for watching his bike even though it was safe in the yard. If I saw him at the store, he'd give me all the change from his pocket. He liked me cuz I was the only one who could beat him at chess. Everyone else would laugh at me when we played chess because I'm a real hard thinker. They'd get mad and tell me I think too much.

Bird wasn't like that; he'd say, "Take yo time."

Morris would laugh and say, "Study long, study wrong."

Bird was a good match for me. Sometimes, I'd beat him, but most times he'd win. He'd say, "You let me win?" I didn't. I swear I didn't. He was just good. He was better than me.

Sometimes my brothers would laugh at me for thinking so hard. I'd play faster without thinking. Bird ain't like it when I played fast like that, because he would win too easy. I was supposed to play chess with him the day before we moved off Herman but, thing is, he got killed right before we moved. It wasn't in no crime or nothin'. He got in a fight with his girlfriend, he beat her bad. She was chasing Bird down Herman Street, her face all bloody like a woman from one of them scary movies. He was running his ass off, but it didn't matter. Thing about her, she ran track for Kensington High School. She was faster than Bird.

She put a knife through his back.

They said he died instantly. He did too, I saw it for myself. We were all out there watching it happen. He just fell to the ground like that time a chestnut tree fell on our landlord Mr. Small's work truck. Bird ain't put his hands out to stop himself or nothin'. He was dead.

After she put the knife through his back she was just standing there with the bloody knife. Ain't nobody hardly notice her, but I did. I saw she was mad and sad at the same time. She let out this real bad scream. Morris said it was "primal."

When they turned Bird over it looked like someone took the energy from his body. All his blood was on the street and he was just…motionless. I kept wanting to cry, but I couldn't. There's a ghetto rule against it. Black boys can't never cry or they a punk if they do. If one of the older dudes catch you crying they'a start saying, "What, you got a little Rick James in you?" Them older dudes always making fun of Rick James, talking about how he dress like a woman and wear his hair like a woman.

Even if you wanna cry, you can't.

Bird died before he hit the ground. They said it wasn't losing all that blood that killed him. They said it was that his girlfriend pulled the knife out after she stabbed him. They said the wound to his heart killed him. They said because she pulled the knife out, his heart couldn't beat no more. They said if she woulda left the knife in, he coulda made it to surgery. They coulda saved him.

They ain't even put her in jail. Elijah said, "They ain't gon' put a woman in jail for killing a black man. They'a put a black man in jail for killing another black man, so they can take two black men out society." They said his murder was "in the heat of passion." I ain't understand it because it wasn't no passion that caused her to kill Bird.

When the police came to check on Cynthia, Mama was still watching through the curtains. "It's late. Go to bed."

"I seen it."

"JuJu, go to bed."

"But I seen it. I seen what happened. We should tell the cops."

"Don't you know better than that? It ain't our business. Now. Sleep. Go."

"I can't. I can't sleep over here. It's always sirens and ambulances and fire trucks and fightin'. How can you sleep? How can anybody normal sleep?"

"You'a get used to it."

"I don't want to. This ain't normal."

Mama gave me her mean eye. "I ain't playin' wit'chu, boy."

I left her for my bedroom.

6

I didn't like Guilford Street. I didn't like the cars speeding by, men throwing cigarette butts out their window. I didn't like the trash in the street. I didn't like the uncut grass. Every lawn I looked on was uncut. Even ours.

When I looked over to Ashley's front yard, I saw a body on the lawn. As I got closer, I saw the body was a woman. She was just lying there, naked. Fully naked. She didn't even have socks on her feet. I stood there looking at her. I thought she was dead. I looked closer. She was breathing.

Kevin came out of his yard. He was excited. "Yo?" He started laughing. "Yo mama out here butt-ass naked." He made this freaky Scooby-doo laugh. "Ashley gon' go crazy if he see you looking at her."

"They don't know she out here like this. Why don't they cover her up?"

"I don't know, but they gon' play around and I'ma fuck this bitch." He rolled his hips in simulation. He groaned, "Yeah."

I didn't know what to think.

"She hoeing," he said. He got closer, inspecting her nakedness. It seemed like he was thinking about climbing on top of her limp, drugged out body.

His father came from Kevin's house and stood behind his son, wearing a Dr. Pepper cap and shirt. He worked driving a truck back and forth to supermarkets, until they caught him stocking women's houses with free pop. That's how he got a divorce from Kevin's mother. He was bigger than his son. Bigger and blacker, with lips that looked like he'd never seen a bottle he didn't like. I could even smell the alcohol on him.

Kevin Sr. smacked his son in the back of the head. He pulled Kevin by the arm. "Boy, get yo ass 'way from here. You'd stand here all day looking at her if you could. G'on and meet one of these little gals 'round here." While he was chastising his son, several boys came and stood around looking at Ashley's naked mother. One of them was Dondon.

"Aye, what's yo name?"

"JuJu."

"I'm Dondon. This my brother Ronron."

"Don'don. Ron'ron. Y'all twins?"

"Yeah. We twins. Fraternal."

"What that mean?"

"Means we're not identical," they said together.

"Oh, alright."

Ronron asked, "Y'all new huh?"

"Nah we lived down here before, 'round the corner on Herman."

Ronron nodded. Then Dondon nodded with him. I smiled.

With all the commotion and chatter I didn't notice the throng standing behind me. Kevin Sr. called, "Vivian?"

Vivian didn't wake. In fact, she didn't move at all. Whatever she took had her on another planet. She was high as a kite.

Kevin Sr. called her again. She didn't respond. Kevin Sr. poked her. Nothing. She still didn't wake when he slapped her. "Vivian, get yo tired ass off these streets. Out here with yo ass all out for these kids to see."

She didn't move.

Kevin Sr. turned to us. "G'on 'way from here now. G'on home. Ain't y'all never seen an ass before. You want to see ass, go bend over in the mirror."

We laughed.

The noise and laughter must have woken the family because the prettiest girl I ever seen came running off the stoop with a blanket. My heart was skipping beats. I could feel the air leaving my nose. I took a deep breath. She was gorgeous. Her skin was a perfect brown cinnamon stick. The thin shirt she wore couldn't hide the perfect firmness inside her bra and her shorts didn't do any justice covering her thighs. When she threw the blanket over her mother, her ass was like a gazelle's. She was perfect. When she looked back to see who was watching, my eyes met hers. She smiled. I was in love.

Ashley came rushing out behind his sister. "Get off my grass. Get the fuck off my grass. I'a fuck you up."

His sister called to him. "Ashley?" His fists were tight. "Ashley, help me," she pleaded.

He backed away. Before he hopped to help his sister, he pointed at me. He didn't say anything.

Ronron laughed. "He always do that."

Dondon added, "Aye. I think I remember you. Sean, yo brother. Right?"

I nodded. "Yeah."

Ronron said, "Yeah I remember. Sean used to be that roller-skating dude, right? He used to ride his bike around here popping wheelies and shit. Him and dude, what's his name?"

"Bird."

"Right. Right. Bird."

"What happened to him? I don't see dude no more."

"Sean? Or Bird?"

"Bird. I ain't seen him in a while."

"He got murdered. Like two, almost three years ago," I said.

"Oh, word."

Dondon asked, "What about Sean?"

"He in juvy."

"Word?"

"Yeah, till he twenty-one."

"Damn. Twenty-one? What he do?"

"He robbed that skating rink in the Thruway Mall."

"Word. I thought he worked there?"

"He did. That's why he in juvy till he twenty-one. White people trusted him. Paid him to skate and teach other people how to skate. He got $20,000 out the safe. You know they make an example outa you for shit like that."

They nodded in unison.

"Yeah."

7

By our second Sunday Mama was telling me, "Go make some friends." I didn't want to. I wanted to walk out my door and see Jenifer or Richard or Henry or Mrs. Shumaker. I wanted to hear everyone talking about our neighbor, Mr. Dean. He was a real weird dude. He drove this old pickup truck like on *Sanford and Son*. When he started it, it sounded like a tractor was running through the backyard.

Mr. Dean worked at Bethlehem Steel. He was older than Mama, real old. He was like fifty-five or something. Even though he was weird and had dead deer hanging in his yard, he was always nice to me and my sisters. When they stopped giving Mama government cheese, and government meat and gravy, and government rice, and government peanut butter, and that government powder milk, Mr. Dean would hunt deer and give Mama some meat.

Sometimes I'd walk past his house and see a deer hanging in his yard, deer blood dripping into a washtub. Mama would get mad at me if I didn't eat no "venison," but I just kept seeing deer eyes whenever I tried to eat it.

This morning I didn't hear Mr. Dean's old truck. I just lay there looking at the ceiling thinking about his old truck and the people on Humboldt Parkway.

One Saturday, Mr. Dean took me and Mama to pick vegetables. He kept asking his sons to go with him but they didn't want to. He said they was "no good," and don't know what it means to "work for a living." In fact, his sons were criminals. All six of them. One of his sons went and cut a hole in the roof of Sattler's department store. He cleaned the place out while everyone slept. Another one of his sons robbed a jewelry store and shot the owner to get away with the jewelry. They put him in Clinton Correctional Facility, and he gon' be in there for twenty-five years. Another one of his sons robbed that bank right there on Broadway and Fillmore. That bank with the big clock on it. None of his sons wanted to pick vegetables. They said, "We ain't slaves no more."

His sons ain't go but Mama did. Mama said she missed Alabama, and she wanted to "work in the fields." Mr. Dean's sons laughed at her. They was calling her a slave. His middle son DJ, who look just like his father said, "You look just like a black ass slave anyway." Mama was sad he said that to her. I could see it in her. She ain't say nothing but I could tell she was mad. When they was leaving, Mr. Dean again asked if anyone wanted to pick vegetables.

I said, "I'll go."

Mama didn't want me to go. "Boy, you ain't gon' pick no tomatoes," she said.

"Let him go. Everybody need to see where they food come from, like we did."

When I got in his truck Mr. Dean said, "All I want to see is yo ass up in them fields. You betta be just like a duck." He laughed.

Mama said, "Don't get out here talkin' yo shit. You hear me?"

We picked tomatoes. It was the hardest thing I ever did in my entire life. They give you this fruit basket and you had to walk to the other side of the field and start picking. Every time you fill a basket you have to walk it all the way back to their truck and they mark an X by your name and count it as twenty-five cents.

When we finished, I made $11.25. Mama made $47.00 and Mr. Dean made $53.50. They picked cucumbers on another Saturday, and cut cabbage after that, but I ain't go with them.

When I was just lying in bed, Mama called me. I came to see what she wanted.

"Go and get a pint of ice cream for dinner."

"Go to Super Duper?"

"No, not no damn Super Duper. Do I got Super Duper money? Go to the store on the corner, boy. The one on Sycamore. They got little pints of ice cream, like this." She showed me how little with her fingers.

We lived closer to Broadway. In order to get to the corner store on Sycamore, I'd have to walk the length of Guilford. I was a little nervous.

When I got outside, I could hear people arguing inside their houses. I could hear people playing music. I could smell all the Sunday dinners. I smelled cinnamon like someone was making peach cobbler and fried chicken and collard greens. Every yard I came on made me look deep into the void hoping no one wanted to rob the two dollars Mama gave me for ice cream. Most yards was empty. Some yards had boys playing up trees or girls jumping rope. One yard I passed, a pitbull ran toward me. My heart was racing. I thought it was gon' get me but it was tied to a chain that didn't let it get out the yard. On one porch I seen a real old lady smiling at me. She looked like she was one hundred years old. Across the street I heard men laughin'. I looked because I thought they was laughing at me being scared of that pitbull. They was just drinking and laughing, enjoying themselves.

When I looked in one yard, I saw two boys fighting. I noticed their mothers were watching, and cheering for a winner. "Beat his ass, Squirt," "Beat his ass, Melvin," their mothers said.

The boys was younger than me. Probably both around ten years old. Melvin was losing.

His mother said, "You better beat his ass or I'ma beat yo ass."

Melvin was trying but Squirt was a better fighter. Melvin looked dejected. I saw in his eyes he didn't want to fight.

Melvin looked at his mother. "He my friend."

His mother said, "You ain't got no friends. Niggas ain't yo friend. I don't know how many times I gotta tell yo ass. None of these niggas give a damn about you. Now, you betta beat his ass." She pushed Melvin back out there.

Melvin wasn't no fighter. He wasn't good enough. I was thinking someone should break it up. If you try to be a peacemaker, they'll say, "If you break it up, I'ma knock yo bitch ass out." So, I watched.

Melvin got knocked to the ground. His mother snatched him back to his feet. "I ain't raise you to be no bitch. My son ain't gon' be no bitch. You better beat his ass, you hear me?"

Tears ran down Melvin's face.

"Fuck is you crying for?" His mother punched him in the chest—hard. I heard it. Melvin's mother said, "Ain't no cryin'. You ain't no bitch. Bitches cry. What kinda black man God gave me? Cryin' like a bitch."

Melvin looked lost at his mother for punching him. All the boys was laughing she called him a bitch. They was pretending to throw her punch at each other.

"Get yo ass to the house," she said.

Melvin got some bravery. "I'ma fight him, Mama."

"You betta win, gotdamnit."

They started again. Melvin was on his back taking a beating. His mother said, "Don't break it up, fuck that!"

Squirt was pounding him.

"Fight back, gotdamnit!" Melvin's mother yelled.

After a minute of beating, Squirt stopped hitting Melvin and walked away. He was flexing his muscles. Melvin's mother picked him off his back. She slapped his face. "Man up. Man the fuck up!" she yelled. The other boys and even some of the men was high-fiving Squirt.

"Boy, that Squirt don't play."

"Squirt be kicking they ass, don't he?"

One man was laughing and drinking. "Goddamn. Goddamn," he said, in what seemed disbelief.

***

When I neared the corner of Guilford and Sycamore, I saw the twins sitting on their porch playing cards. I crossed and talked to them for a minute.

"What up?"

"Wanna play Uno?" they asked.

I told them I'd come back after I go to the store for Mama.

The twins was cool. They came from a good family. Their grandparents was retired. Their mother was in a nursing program. I never met their father. Their grandfather was a tough old dude, though. He got mad at us because we stole cherries out the cherry tree, behind their house. The tree wasn't in their yard but if you climbed their gate you could get into the cherry tree without going into their neighbor's yard. "Stay out them people tree, you hear me?" he said.

They said, "Yes sir."

He looked at me.

"Yes. Sir."

We didn't listen though. I mean I woulda listened but Chill came down talking about he hungry. Before I knew it, the four of us was in that cherry tree. I was so far up in the canopy of that cherry tree my leg was shaking real bad. I got dizzy, thinking I was gon' fall. I was trying to put cherries in a Super-Duper bag and I just lost my footing.

I thought I was gon' die. I thought I was gon' hit the ground and make a big splat.

I was holding on. I saw the twins run. I thought they was gon' sit on they porch and say they had nothing to do with my death. They came back with their grandfather.

"I told y'all to stay off that goddamn tree, didn't I?"

I heard the twins say, "Yes sir."

Their old grandfather rushed off. I thought he was gon' leave me hanging by the branch I caught onto. He came back with a ladder.

When I got down, I was so happy until their grandfather put his old hands around the back of my neck. He made me take him to Mama. Ashley and Kevin was laughing as we passed Ashley's stoop.

Ashley said, "Pop strong as hell, ain't he?"

They was laughing hard.

Marquis came to the door. "What happened?" He started laughing too when he seen that old grandfather with his hand around the back of my neck.

When I got Mama, he told her how I was stealing cherries. Mama was mad, not because I was stealing cherries, but because she was embarrassed.

"JuJu, I coulda bought you some cherries."

I was thinking, *But why didn't you?* I ain't say nothing. I just looked at the floor. That old grandfather picked up my chin.

They talked for a minute. "He like'ta fell to the ground. Woulda been bad." He started telling how he broke his arm falling out a tree when he was little.

Mama liked his story because he was from Mississippi, and all them old stories about picking nuts and fruit out the tree is right up Mama alley. Mama said, "We used to have the best…"

I walked away.

Mama said, "Get yo disrespectful black ass back here. We ain't done talking."

I had to stand there for nearly two hours and listen to them talk about sharecropping, real food, farming, fruit trees, fresh milk, and how "you can't get no fresh figs in the north." They also talked about fishing and snakes and insects. They just kept talking and talking. When they finished Mama told me I couldn't go outside.

"You got school tomorrow."

At dinner, I was telling them about that fight I seen between Melvin and Squirt. Mama said, "Leave them gotdamn people alone. I'm not gon' be out here fighting these crazy motha fuckas. Leave all these crazy motha fuckas alone, fo they hurt one of us. Mind yo gotdamn business. You can't change the world, JuJu. It don't belong to you."

8

Just after the school year ended, I was sitting on my porch listening to my Walkman. My sisters didn't want to walk on Humboldt Parkway with me. Boo said she was sick, so I didn't go. Ashley's crew passed saying, "What up?"

"Where y'all headed?" I asked.

Dondon nodded. "Up the street."

Ronron said, "You comin'?"

Ashley said, "Nope, not him. Not Mama's good boy."

They was laughing.

When I got off the porch my middle sisters scolded, "You can't leave. I'm telling Mama if you leave."

I didn't care. You can't never let them put no brand on you like that. *Mama's good boy.* They always trying to find ways to elevate themselves above you. I had to prove I wasn't no mama's boy. Most boys down here don't want to be taking no instruction from adults. Especially not from they mama. Boys down here raise themselves.

I was quickly off Guilford, following Ashley and his boys across Broadway. We went into Webbers. When we lived on Herman, Webbers was just a Laundromat where you'd find poor people doing laundry. If you paid attention, you'd see junkies putting microdots on their tongue, or snorting a mound of cocaine off the back of their hand. Or you'd see husbands caressing their neighbor's wife, or you'd see teens sneaking into the laundry to find a make-out corner. Even Irish loan sharks had wooden chairs taking and giving cash right out of the laundry. Today, Webbers is a Laundromat, drycleaners, game room, and corner store. People from the neighborhood shop at Webbers for bread and milk and chips and pop and lunchmeat and all kinds of candy and cookies. They also play lotto, buy loose diapers, loose cigarettes, and rolling paper. Nowadays, every boy in the neighborhood goes to Webbers to hang out and play *Super Mario Bros* or *Ms. Pac Man* or *Millipede.*

When we entered Webbers, there was a crowd around *Super Mario Bros.* Kevin smacked his teeth.

Under his breath, Ashley uttered, "This dude."

I could feel the tension.

His friends was yelling, "Yeah, Tone. Do that shit, Tone."

I didn't know him. Dondon said he was almost eighteen. Said he was still in tenth grade. Said his family moved out of the Perry Housing Projects last year. Said he lived on Coit Street. They said when Tone moved on Coit, "he walked up to Earl and punched him square in the face." Earl been his flunky ever since. They're thieves, pickpockets, and purse snatchers. They said he tried to get Ashley on his side, but Ashley didn't like his demanding style, or the fact that Tone would take half the earnings for himself. When Ashley refused to be his underling, Tone and Ashley became enemies. Ashley and his boys stayed on our side of Broadway, except to play *Super Mario Bros.* Tone kept it like that until he got into *Super Mario Bros.* Now he don't want us even in Webbers because it's on his side of Broadway. We go anyway.

Ashley and the crew was making their presences felt. Clearing their throat. Shifting. Crossing and uncrossing their arms.

Earl looked at us real hard. We ain't move. Tone ain't never take his attention off *Super Mario Bros.* I thought there might be a fight. There wasn't. We waited for another minute. I couldn't see the screen, but I could see Ashley inhale and exhale big sighs.

"Let's get out of here," he said.

Kevin pleaded, "He almost on the Everlasting."

"You can stay. I ain't watching this fool."

We left Webbers and wandered aimlessly. We walked up Broadway toward the Broadway Market. All the white people watched us like we were going to start some trouble. It was like they knew we were trouble, even if I didn't.

***

Broadway is divided. Half of it—the half before Fillmore Avenue—is mostly black. The other half—after Fillmore—is mostly white. Buffalo is segregated like that. Then you have streets controlled by different black boys, like Tone controls Coit. Someone else controls Reed Street and someone else Herman Street, and so on. The toughest dude on Guilford was this boy named Man. He's the reason Tone never could get too far with Ashley. If Tone wanted to control Guilford, he'd have to deal with the older boys like Man. Man went to prison so now it's Morris that Tone would have to deal with. Morris don't control Guilford though, everyone just knows his Mama live there, so they leave us alone.

The white half of Broadway is inhabited by Polish, Russian, and German poor. They surround the Broadway Market between Fillmore and Bailey Avenues. The white half of Broadway is protected by a small police station where police cars patrol Fillmore and Broadway, keeping blacks from intruding too far into the white neighborhoods. If you are coming into the white section, you do so for shopping or banking or employment or some business that has you in the white section for as long as it takes you to handle your business, or be questioned for loitering. If you are walking to go to the nice community center for white people, you have to do so with your eyes down. If you notice too much, the police stop you. They think you're planning a crime if you're noticing too much. If you late and you start running, the police watch you like you committed a crime. They'll stop you and say, "Well, you were running."

When I was seven, the police picked up Sean and me for walking in the street. The snow was to my knee on the sidewalk. Sean hated cops. They just pulled up and rolled down their window.

"Get out the street."

"Ain't nowhere to walk," Sean said.

"The sidewalk. Hear of it?"

"Snow this high."

They crept beside us. "Hey. Walk on the gotdamn sidewalk. Now."

Sean let out a puff. "We just walkin'. We ain't committing no crimes."

They stopped. We didn't. The passenger got out. "Come here. Come here. Okay, tough guy."

The driver got out with a breath of steam like he was a dragon. The passenger had his fist balled in Sean's coat.

"I told you to walk on the gotdamn sidewalk. You blacks always wanna be tough."

"Always a tough guy," his partner said.

Sean wasn't even being tough. He was just standing limp around the cop's fist. I was thinkin' they was gon' beat Sean. Cops always trying to show black boys they tougher than us.

"You wanna be tough? Get in."

They forced us in the backseat and drove us seven or eight blocks. I was scared. I thought maybe they'd kill us and nobody would know about it. I was cryin'. Sean was shaking his head.

"Don't," he whispered.

Police always saying we acting tough even when we ain't. Sean ain't even no fighter, he a thief.

They stopped the car. There was a little patch that was shoveled in front of a deli, the only patch shoveled on the entire sidewalk. "See right here. Walk on the sidewalk."

They rode next to us as we trudged through knee-high snow. Sean had to lift me up one time because a drift was higher than my hip. When I was on his back Sean said, "Don't never cry in front of them. They want to break you. Don't let 'em. We ain't do nothin' wrong. Plus, black men don't cry. You hear me?"

"Mhmm."

It's always like that. Police watch you like you're not American, from the time they get you in their sight. The entire ghetto is set up like that, with police stations encircling the ghetto. Outside the ring of police stations is all the nice houses white people live in. Outside the circle of police is America. The America they tell you about in politics and on TV. White people want you to know where you can walk and where you can shop and eat and live. They call the cops on you if you outside that circle of police, set up to protect whites from us bad blacks. It don't feel like you're an American when you live in the ghetto. It feel like they want to see yo freedom papers.

The cops don't come to protect and serve. They come asking, "What you doing in this neighborhood? Where you going? Where do you live? Is this yo car? Where you coming from?" The police come with the intent to protect white people from you. They come with force and scowls and fists and hands on guns. They come like they gon' tackle you, or worse.

White people try to restrict your movements if you outside the ghetto. The police give you criminal infractions or large traffic tickets. They try to reinforce your behavior and after so many arrests or tickets or close calls with the police, you start to believe you belong in the ghetto.

In school the teachers say you're free and Lincoln emancipated the slaves. They tell you about freedom and Dr. King. They tell you how America is a free country. Then when you ain't in school learning about American freedom, white people put all these rules on you. Rules on where you belong and how long you can be there. Rules on where you can walk and shop and play. That's not what Dr. King died for. That's not American. That's not freedom.

9

We went into the Broadway Market. It was filled with all kinds of meats and cheeses and sweets we could never afford. There was booths filled with fresh cakes and pies and Eastern European treats. Food was stacked and layered and hanging. Not that rotted stuff they sell in the ghetto. In the ghetto they sell rotted food in the supermarkets. It ain't good like this food in the Broadway Market. My mouth started watering.

All the supermarkets in the white neighborhood have all the best food in them. They have all the fresh fruit and meat. Mama said, "When the food go old, they ship it down to the ghetto with a new label on it." Mama was convinced that was true. Especially if her fruit went bad after a couple days. One time she peeled the label off some chicken wings and it was another label under it. Mama took it right back to Super-Duper. She was mad they wouldn't return her money so she threw the entire package on the floor and left. "I'm not feeding my kids this rotted shit." Mama was convinced all the food in the ghetto was rotted. One time, I seen her mash her thumb in rotted peaches, so no one would buy them. She would do that to all the rotted fruit and vegetables.

White people build all the good supermarkets outside the ghetto and if you want to get to one you have to go through a ring of police just waiting to pull you over. Elijah said, "They be wanting to give black people tickets so taxes go down on them big houses they built."

In the good supermarket, I could sense white people watching us. They always make you feel like you don't belong. My heart was beating so bad. It felt like they was always watching and judging and telling how I was a bad black, even if they ain't know me. I ain't want to be surrounded by so many white people. I wanted to turn and run. They was just watching me like I was a runaway slave.

Being a black boy is strange. Inside, I'm just JuJu. I just want to play arcade games and hang out with my friends. Outside, I'm a six-foot-tall, 140-pound black man. People treat me different. They scared of me. I'm a threat to them.

It just happens one day. You don't even have time to become a man. One day they just change. They don't look at you the same. I can see it in their eyes, all of them. Mama. My teachers. Police officers. Old black people. White people. It's a hard transition to make. You think it'll always be like it was before you became their threat, but it ain't. They get you in trouble. They call the cops on you. They treat you like you have to be taught a good lesson on who's runnin' things. On where you belong. They treat you like you have to be broken.

We followed Ashley to a bulk candy section in the middle of the Broadway Market. Kevin, Chill, and the twins walked through aisles of wine barrels filled with bulk candy saying which candy they'd buy if they had money. Then I noticed something. Whenever they'd point at what they wished they could buy, they'd use their other hand to grab a fistful of candy and put it into their pocket. I didn't take any candy.

Ashley was watching me. He nodded—a command. You steal or you don't belong.

I didn't want to be an outsider. I didn't want them to get a word out on me, a word that I was a coward. That I was lame.

I took a handful and hurried it in my pocket. I was both scared and ashamed. I did it anyway.

Ashley smiled.

I wasn't excited about it. It felt like I'd done exactly what everybody thought I would. I had to. I couldn't think about consequences. I had to live down here.

When we exited, we used the back door that led to the parking garage. They was laughing over our haul, and I was laughing with them. I was too far into it. Sometimes it just happens like that. It's just the pressure of the environment. That, and if you don't participate, they start treating you funny. They start to distance themselves from you. Worst thing you can be in the ghetto is an outsider.

A group of white boys was riding skateboards down the parking ramp. Ashley and the crew were counting who had the most candy. They turned to me. "What'chu get?"

I showed a handful.

"Nice for your first time."

When we were trading flavors, a white boy skated over to us. "That's all y'all got? We go in the back door and get a bag full." He opened the school bag he carried over his shoulder, full of candy. I could see Ashley's eyes light up. Another white boy yelled, "Security!"

Everyone took off. The white boys rode off on their skateboards, giving the guards the finger. Until that moment, I didn't know the Broadway Market had guards.

Kevin was a mile out in front of us. He was fast. We hit Paderewski Drive, then a left on Sears Street, so that we was back on Broadway. Kevin musta knew where we was going because we were right where we wanted to be. When Kevin stopped running, he sat on the steps of the Polish Community Center. We caught up and everyone laughed over it.

While we were crossing Fillmore, Kevin stopped. "Yo, I'm 'bout to go to my Mama house."

Ashley said, "I'm comin'."

The twins said they had to get home.

Ashley joked, "G'on home, Mama's boy."

"Man, shut up…" Dondon said.

Ronron added, "You always talking shit."

Chill followed them. I followed Ashley and Kevin to his mother's house.

Kevin's mother lived on Wilson Street, just inside Fillmore. His mother had a one and a half story shack like the one we rented at 99 Guilford Street. It was bigger than the one-bedroom apartment his father rented.

Kevin went inside telling us to wait for him on the porch. As soon as Ashley and I sat on the banisters, I could hear his mother yelling.

"Asshole. Stupid asshole!"

Apparently, Kevin stayed away too long, preventing her from having a babysitter. She said she'd be short in her paycheck, and it was his fault.

"You. Dumb. Black. Motha fucka. You just like yo no good, drunk ass daddy. You don't do shit in school. I swear, Kevin. I swear to God, if you ain't gon' do shit in school, if you ain't gon' get no job, and if you ain't gon' watch yo brothers, don't come back. I mean it. I mean that shit, Kevin. You don't even play football no more. If you ain't gon' help me around the house, then don't bring yo black ass back, you hear me?"

Every time she called Kevin a "black motha fucka," Ashley grabbed my arm and laughed like Richard Pryor was telling jokes. I heard the same from my mother in some form or another. Parents in the ghetto always telling you that you like some no-good they know or like the bad parent they no longer with. Mama always say that to me, if she mad. That I'm just like my daddy. My daddy supposed to be a no-good, womanizing, adultering bastard. According to Mama, I'm just like him.

Kevin kept saying, "I'm sorry, Mama. Mama, I'm sorry."

She was irate. "You just like that motha fucka. Just like his ass for the world. Gotdamn, I don't know what I was thinking when I met his ugly ass. Why me, God? Ain't no dick this good."

"I'm sorry, Mama. I be working all the time, Mama. I be mopping and taking out trash at Alphonso's."

"Get yo shit, and don't come back. If you ain't gon' watch your brothers while I work, gotdamnit, don't come back."

It got quiet. Ashley whispered, "Yo, one day I was in they house and they had a chain on the fridge so Kevin wouldn't eat all they food. And a lock so he couldn't take it off."

"Oh, that's why he stay with his father?"

"Nah, he stay with his father cuz his stepfather kick his ass all the time. One time his stepfather made him go out on the porch while they ate dinner."

Ashley thought it was funny. He nodded our silence as Kevin came to the door. "Yo? They said my Mama can work the nightshift. I'ma stay over here."

When I got home it was well after the time Mama usually came home from her laundry job. Usually she'd be home by 4:30. I didn't see her car in the driveway. When I looked to the porch, I saw my youngest sister in the window with a face full of tears. I told Ashley I was going in.

"You comin' back out?"

"I don't know."

10

When I got inside my youngest sister Kimerlee, who is seven, cried out, "When Mama coming home?"

"I don't know. Why you cryin'?"

"Cuz Mama ain't come home."

"I'm sure she alright."

"How you know? She supposed to come home. You remember when that man tried to kidnap me?"

"Mama fine. She can take care of herself. She probably got a new job."

I showed her a palmful of candy from my pocket.

"Where you get penny candy from?"

"Do you want it?"

"Yeah."

She took a Mary Jane, a Bit-O-Honey, and a hard lemon ball from my palm.

"Did you eat?"

"No. Boo said she ain't cooking nothin' because she not my mama, then she went in her room and put on her Walkman."

Boo is the oldest of my three sisters. She's twelve. She was born sick. Last winter she got sick real bad. I mean, she been getting sick since she was two, but it was real bad last year. Mama was scared because Boo's doctor said, "If she doesn't improve by morning, we'll have to put her on life support."

Mama asked, "Can this kill her?"

He nodded. "It's very serious."

When Mama was working, we had a snowball war versus the other side of Humboldt Parkway. The blizzard came overnight and covered everything. The snow was up to my hip. We didn't even have school for a couple of days. I didn't mind it. I made snowmen with my sisters. We threw snowballs at each other. One time they jumped on me and pushed me face-first into a snowdrift. Boo couldn't play in the snow as much as we could. Sometimes I'd see her watching from her bedroom. Sometimes I'd make a snowball and bring it to her. Once when I turned to leave, she hit me in the head with it. I didn't get mad or nothin'.

She wanted to be out with everybody else—and I tried to stop her, I swear I did—but she wouldn't listen. I made her put on more clothes than anybody. She even wore Morris' ski mask. She was covered from head to toe. Her eyes was the only part of her uncovered.

We stayed out all day throwing snowballs. When Mama got home from work, Boo could barely make it in the house.

"Y'all been out here all day?" Mama looked at me like I knew better. "JuJu?" When Mama took off Boo's ski mask her eyes swelled shut. It was the scariest thing I ever seen.

She cried, "I can't see, Mama. I can't see."

Mama was mad at me. "I told you to stay in the gotdamn house!"

Whenever we visited Boo, I would just look out the window, watching the snow. I couldn't hardly look at Boo without thinking it was my fault. I used the metro to visit her all the time when she started getting better, and Mama would get mad because my two youngest sisters Terah and Kimerlee would be home alone, or alone with Elijah. She'd say I can't leave them like that.

"Be there with them, gotdamnit!"

After Boo's eyes swelled, we'd stay in the house when Mama was working. If Mama was home, she'd play Ella Fitzgerald's Christmas album, even while we was watching TV. Mama was always making us hot chocolate. She'd always get us cinnamon rolls from Bells on her way home. Sometimes Boo would have to sit in front of the oven because she was cold. I would get a chair and sit with her. She was always telling me about the books she read. They would give her a lot of books in the children's hospital, because Mama couldn't afford to get her a TV. I started reading with her the year before. I told her I was gon' write a book when I get grown and she believed me too.

"It's gon' be good and everybody gon' love it because you is smart, JuJu."

Boo got better over time. She was even riding her bike again, yesterday. She just don't like cookin'.

"Okay, what'd you want to eat?" I asked Kimerlee.

Kimerlee said, "Lasagna or spaghetti."

I smiled. "I can't make lasagna, or spaghetti. Let's see what we got." I opened the fridge. "What about bologna?"

"No, I don't want bologna."

"What if I fry it and put some cheese on it?"

"No. I don't want bologna. Plus, ain't no bread."

She was right. I opened the cupboard. There was three cans of Spaghetti-Os, a box of oatmeal, and a box of grits in there.

"What about Spaghetti-Os?"

"Okay, but it's not like the spaghetti Mama make."

"Well, Mama not here."

When I was eating with Kimerlee, the other two came into the kitchen.

Boo said, "Why you ain't make me none?"

The middle of the three, Terah, who is nine, said, "And why you ain't put no cheese in it?"

Kimerlee said, "I don't like cheese in my Spaghetti-Os."

"Y'all was here all day and y'all could have cooked Spaghetti-Os with cheese while I was gone."

Terah didn't like my answer. "I'm telling Mama if you don't cook me none."

So, I made two more cans of Spaghetti-Os, this time with cheese melted in.

The four of us ate Spaghetti-Os at the kitchen table, me and my sisters. When we were done, my sisters crowded the couch watching TV and eating stolen candy.

From the kitchen, I heard Boo say, "This is my pillow. It's for one butt. This is your pillow, it's for your butt."

Terah called, "You ain't watching *The Cosby Show* with us, JuJu?"

"Yes I am."

I was gon' watch with them right after I ate like five pieces of bologna. We was always watching *The Cosby Show*, wishing we had a life like that. I was always thinking I could be like Dr. Huxtable, if I had a different life. If my father woulda been here we coulda had a better life. They was both hardworking and we coulda owned the best house on Humboldt Parkway, if they was together. I coulda went to a better school and got better grades. I coulda went to college and married a smart black woman and never came back to the ghetto.

Whenever I looked at my sisters they was laughing and enjoying the show. They was laughing too hard.

"What was that funny?"

Terah said, "We ain't laughing at that."

"What then?"

I could tell they was making a joke on me. They was sneaking and whispering and being annoying.

Terah blurted, "You got a big ole Bill Cosby head."

I ain't even get mad. I mean I did, but it was good to see Boo laughing. We laughed and listened and dreamed through the entire show.

After I came back from the bathroom, I saw Kimerlee in the window again.

"You ain't sleepy?"

"No. I want to wait for Mama."

I knew this was trouble. Whenever she wanted to wait for Mama, she was up all night. One time she fell asleep right under the window and Mama got mad at me because she didn't sleep in her bed. I knew I was gon' be up all night with her. I sat on the floor with my back to the window and tried to reason with her.

"In the morning when you wake up, Mama will be here. You should go to sleep."

"I don't want to. I wanna wait for Mama."

"Why?"

"Because."

I took a breath.

"She ain't kiss me good night."

It was nearly midnight. Kimerlee didn't want to do anything except stand in the window waiting for Mama to come home from work. She was crying again. I'd given her all the candy from my pocket, but she wouldn't leave the window.

"Is that Mama?"

A car drove by. It was maybe the tenth time she asked if the car was Mama's.

"No. It's not Mama. Mama has a small car. She has a Ford Maverick. That's a big car. Looks like one of those Buick Electras. You know like the one Teddy drives." Teddy was one of Mama's friends.

"Oh, is that Teddy?"

"Probably not. Everyone drives those now."

It must have been well past midnight before she was tired enough to leave the window. I told her if she went to bed, Mama would bring her donuts from Freddie's for breakfast.

"And some milk?"

I nodded. "Yep, and *chocolate* milk."

She was happy. She agreed and finally made it into her bunkbed over Terah. Their bedroom was off the dining room, right next door to Mama's, which was off the living room. Boo had a bedroom near the kitchen, and her door was always shut. There were two bedrooms on the second floor—mine, and one with twin beds for my jailbird brothers.

When it was quiet and my sisters were sleeping, I went to bed. It musta been around 2:00 before I closed my eyes.

***

In the morning, when I left the heat of my bedroom, I did so for the smell of Mama's breakfast. Mama was making pancakes. Her friend Martin was in the kitchen with her and my sisters. They tried to date one time but Martin tell everyone Mama his sister now.

Kimerlee remembered the donuts. "JuJu said you was gon' get me some donuts from Freddie's."

Mama looked at me. "Why'd you tell her that?"

I slammed my back teeth together, tightening my jaw so I wouldn't tell the truth.

"Uh-oh." Mama always say that when she thinks I'm angry. Once she said I was an "ornery sonovabitch who don't like people, just like yo father."

A couple days ago, Mama was talking to this lady named Ajax she works with at her laundry job. Ajax was teaching Mama how to make rice crispy treats. My sisters said "Hi" and pretended to be interested. I didn't say nothin'. Not one word.

Mama said, "Say hi, JuJu."

I said, "Bump hi."

Mama slapped me. "You bet not never say something like that to me as long as you live, boy. You hear me?"

Apparently, the word "bump" was too close to the real thing. I didn't want to go, so I was ornery. I wanted to hang out with my new friends.

While she was flipping pancakes, Mama said, "Why you mad now?"

"I'm not mad."

"Martin is just my friend, that all."

I didn't understand what she meant.

He looked at me, correcting Mama. "Uncle Martin."

Mama continued, "Your father lied to me. It's his fault. Not mine. Not yours. His."

Boo looked at me with crazy eyes. I smirked. We had our own conversation without talking.

Mama went back to pouring sizzling pancake batter. "Guess what?" she said. "I went to a baseball game last night. In Toronto. What's they name?"

Martin sang, "Blue Jays. Blue jay, fly away blue jay."

I could tell he was drinking his breakfast.

"It was so nice and the hot dogs was so good. And they had this pretzel with this spicy cheese… I'ma get y'all some one day."

I didn't want to hear her stories. I went out on the porch. When I was walking out the door, I heard Mama say, "Let him go. He always angry. He blames me."

I must have sat on the porch watching traffic for an hour. Terah came and asked if I wanted pancakes, which she always pronounced, *pan-a-cakes.*

"It's only three left, you better get it before we eat it."

When I went inside, Martin said, "A 'der JuJu, I'm 'bout to ride off to da sunset. I'a check you out lader." With that, he left on Mama's old ten-speed.

11

I was supposed to go to the grocery store with a $20 bill that Mama taped to the TV screen. I knew Mama wasn't coming home for a while. I knew this because Elijah came looking for Mama every day this week. When I'd open the door for him, he'd say, "Y'all ain't seen her, huh?"

I'd say, "She at work," and he'd give me a grimace like it wasn't true.

Mama would do this from time to time, especially if she was seeing someone new.

One day, Elijah brought us a box of Hostess snack cakes and a box of iced oatmeal cookies he got from the Hostess Bakery Thrift Store on Ferguson and Barthel. Another day he got us some hot dogs, buns, pickles, and potato chips. I knew when Mama taped that twenty on the TV, it meant we were on our own for a while. It'd been like that since my father left. From time to time she just went off on her own like she's single. I mean, unless she working three jobs. If she working three jobs, we still didn't see her, only it's because she working. She ain't been working three jobs since we moved so I knew she was gone because she had a new boyfriend.

Me, Ashley, and Kevin was walking up Broadway. I was supposed to get my sisters some lunch meat and bread and chips and a gallon of Upstate Farms grape drink. I would usually have enough left over for bulk candy or a couple donuts.

That's what I was supposed to do. Instead, I walked past Super Duper, with Ashley and Kevin.

Ashley said, "Come to Payless with me, right quick."

"I gotta go to Super Duper."

"I'm sayin', in and out, real quick."

I thought to myself, *I'll go to Payless with them, then they'll go to Super Duper with me.*

It didn't happen like that.

When we got into Payless, Ashley and Kevin were all smiles. We went into an aisle looking at sneakers. Ashley kept smiling. I couldn't put my finger on his smile, until it was too late.

Ashley said, "What size you wear?"

"Me? Eleven. Why?"

They looked at each other. They was both smiling.

"Tell the lady you want a ten and a half."

"What? Why?"

"Just do it."

I looked at Kevin and he was nodding.

I did it. I don't know why, but I did. I went to the lady behind the counter.

"You boys need any help?"

I held up the sneaker. "Ten and a half?"

She helped me get a ten and a half.

"Here, try them on."

I didn't want to buy sneakers. I didn't have money for sneakers. I was supposed to buy my sisters something to eat. *They're probably waiting for me. They're probably hungry.*

In the mirror, I saw Ashley and Kevin putting on new sneakers. I could see them putting their old sneakers in new boxes. They put the boxes with their old sneakers inside, back on the shelf.

The lady kept trying to get the ten and a half on my foot.

"You might wear an eleven."

"Oh… Yeah. I think I need an eleven now."

When the lady was getting elevens, Ashley and Kevin took off running. She kept looking at me, blaming me with her eyes. I put my old sneakers on.

"I don't want those. I'm sorry."

When I got to the door, she was looking in them boxes with the old sneakers in them.

"Hey, wait. Hey?"

I took off running.

"I'm calling the police."

I ran. I ain't see Kevin or Ashley. They musta made it home. They musta hit a shortcut I didn't know about. I don't know where they went but they was gone. I stopped running. I had to. If you running away from the stores in the white neighborhood the cops think you a crook, even if you ain't.

I shoulda kept running. A cop car pulled up on the side of me. I was walking with my head down, not looking at nobody. I wasn't making no eye contact. I was trying to cross Fillmore and be safely back in the neighborhood.

My heart was beating fast. I tried to ignore him. I tried to act like I ain't see him. I was scared. It was hot. It was already hot when we went inside but when that cop was looking at me it felt like the sun was floating right next to me.

He put his lights on. I kept walking. His car made a *woop woop* sound. I kept walking.

"Hey," he yelled.

When I looked, he said, "Stop."

"Me?"

He pointed his finger to my eye. "You. Stop," he said.

I was thinking about running. Man, I was thinking about it. *Just run*, my mind said. I swear I wanted to run, but I didn't. I didn't because I'm afraid of cops. I have been since I was little. I used to dream they were going to kill me. Mama told us about how they killed her brother back in Alabama, when she was little. All the adults had stories about how someone was killed by the police. "And then they just killed him. He ain't even do nothin'."

I was scared of that siren they have. When we lived on Herman, whenever you heard that siren it meant somebody was dead. Most people in the ghetto don't even call the cops unless somebody been hurt real bad. When I was at the basketball court in Sperry Park, getting a free lunch with Morris and my sisters, the cops came with what seemed like ten thousand cars. They was just jumping out of their cars throwing dudes to the ground. They beat the shit out of this dude named Nathen, because he wouldn't let them throw him to the ground. They just beat him right there in the park. He didn't even do nothing wrong. Morris told us we had to leave before it was us they beat. Them sirens was going real good and they was looking at me like I was a witness. I ain't see nothin'. I looked away.

It's what the cops do, my father told me. He said if you look at a police officer, they'a arrest you for "menacing." Half the black men he knew been arrested for "menacing," he said, but Morris said they don't do that no more.

"They can't charge you for no menacing, just for looking at a white man no more. That's what they used to do. If you look a white man in the eye. Menacing. Ain't no more colored fountains. Now they get you for something else. Now they get you for resisting. Even if you ain't resist. They charged my man Scooter with resisting without violence. How you resist without violence?"

But they both said, "Mind yo business. Or they'a find a reason to arrest you."

My father was part of the reason I was scared of the police. Them bad dreams I had about the police started after I was at the grocery store with my mother and father, when I was five years old. My father mistakenly placed a pack of playing cards in his jacket. He was arguing with Mama over her night job. He didn't want Mama to work overnight. He musta forgot about the playing cards during their heated argument. The cops beat him. They didn't even arrest him. I was crying real bad. I thought they was gon' kill him, but they just left him bloody and confused. He smiled at me as he sat on the floor bloodied.

After a while I stopped crying over it but my heart would beat real fast when their sirens sounded.

When that cop pulled me over, I don't think I could run even if I wanted to. I was shaking. My heart was going crazy. I mean it really beat hard. Beating. Beating. Beating. It was beating so hard I could feel it in my eyes.

The officer kept looking at my feet. Mama told me many times about how nice I had to be to the cops and how I have to be "good natured," and keep my hands out in front of me, but I was still scared. You forget all that stuff yo Mama tell you when they standing right in front of you. You be thinking about survival. Yo mind be telling you to run and get away from them.

Cops don't understand they make you want to run, even if you innocent. They never understand the fear you have of them. They always stand there looking mean saying, "Don't lie to me." That's the one thing cops never understand about being a black boy. They make you fear them. Then they want you to trust them. They say, "I ain't gon' beat you, man. I ain't gon' hurt you. Just tell me the truth. I ain't gon' even lock you up if you tell me you did it." They always be lying and trying to trick you into saying it was you, even if it wasn't. They always standing there with their hands on their gun, all tall and powerful like you supposed to shrink into a little bitty ball in front of them. They ain't friendly like they tell white people. They be trying to make you understand they in charge of the ghetto and you only living cuz they showed you some undeserving mercy.

One time on Herman they chased this dude Dre and when he saw he wasn't gon' get away, he stopped. When he turned, he had a plyer in his pocket. The police tried to tell his mother how he lucky to be alive and how they should be thanking God they didn't kill him. His mother was mad.

"What'd you mean we should thank God? You're not supposed to kill someone over a plyer. What's wrong with you?"

That's how they are. They make you fear them. They make you not want to talk to them. That how it is to be a black boy with the cops. They beat you up then say, "I ain't gon' beat you up." They beat you when you on the ground and holler, "Stop resisting" in their radio, so they'll have a record to say they beat you because you was resisting, even if you wasn't. They say, "Tell me the truth and I ain't gon' lock you up," then they lock you up for telling the truth.

Then if white people looking, they treat you real nice and call you sir so white people can keep believing the cops some good people out to "protect and serve." Well they not. When they enter the ghetto, they ain't nice for shit. I don't know what they like at home, but in the streets, they be looking for action. They be challenging tough guys to fights. They be trying to establish their dominance over the ghetto. They be telling you, "This my corner. I don't want you on my corner."

I was already fearful. The damage is already done for me. I'm scared of them, even the black ones. Normally, I woulda ran. I woulda. But, I didn't. I didn't because I was new and I didn't know all the good spots to hide from the police yet. Plus, I didn't do anything.

He was walking toward me with his hand on his gun. "You been in Payless?"

"Me?"

"You. You was in there, right?"

"Yes. Yes sir." I kept looking at his hand on his gun.

"You steal some sneakers?"

"No. I ain't steal nothin', Officer."

"What about your friends?" He just kept holding on to that gun like it was one of them Wonder Woman truth ropes. Like I would be so scared I wouldn't lie to him.

"I just moved over here from Humboldt Parkway, because Mama lost her night job. I ain't even no bad kid like that, Officer."

He kept looking at me. He kept his hand on his gun. He didn't believe me, I could tell. He looked at my sneakers. "Those boys, you know them?"

"I only been over here for a week or two."

"What's their names?"

Man, my heart was beating bad. "I'm telling you I ain't do it."

"That wasn't my question. You know distracting the clerk is a crime, don't you?"

I didn't know what to say. I still had to live next door to Ashley and Kevin. I didn't want to go to jail for something I didn't do. It was a no-win situation for me.

"I ain't distract the clerk. My mama gave me twenty dollars. I ain't do nothin'. I swear to God I didn't. I knew y'all would blame me, so I left before y'all could." I took the twenty out my pocket to prove I wasn't lying.

The officer nodded. He took his hand off his gun. "I still want their names."

I took a breath.

"It's okay, just tell me their names and I'll let you go."

I felt like he was tricking me. I kept thinking if I tell him their names, he'll say I helped them steal them sneakers, when I didn't. Besides, I couldn't tell him their names even if I wanted to. How could I? Every boy in the ghetto would fight me if I came home with the police.

"What's their names?"

I was trying to think of something. Then it started coming out. "The big one, everybody says his name is Fats." I don't know where I pulled that from. "They be calling him Fat Albert."

"So, his name could be Albert?"

"Huh? I guess so, Officer."

"And the other one?"

I couldn't think. I couldn't breathe. I was shaking real bad. I was trying to hide my shaking. I think he seen me shaking. I ain't want to shake in front of him because black men ain't supposed to be scared.

He was standing over me all burly. I couldn't look him in the eye. I kept looking to the ground. I couldn't think of names. I was scared.

"I'm giving you a break. Give me his name."

The only names I could think of were the ones that came from *To Kill a Mockingbird*. I read it a lot of times. Morris said I was a nerd for reading it. He dropped out of high school so I don't listen to him about stuff like that. Besides, I ain't no nerd. I just like stories that let me think about having a different life.

The officer was looking at me real hard. "What's his name?"

"I think it's Lee."

"And where do they live?"

"I think they stay on Fox Street, Officer. No, maybe Sherman."

"And what's your name?"

"My name? My name is JuJu. Well, people call me JuJu. My name is Julian Stewart, Junior."

The officer let me go after he questioned me. Man, it felt like I won the lotto. I ain't get beat or arrested or nothin'.

12

When I was trying to figure out what to do with myself, Terah called, "JuJu? Somebody want you at the door."

When I got to the door, it was Ashley. "Yo, you comin' out?" He was real happy I ain't tell on him for stealing them sneakers.

We sat on Ashley's stoop for what seemed like hours, just talking. His sister came to the door.

"Ashley, come eat."

He stood to go inside. "You comin' in?"

When we got inside there was an old lady sitting in a chair for old people.

"JuJu, this my gran'ma."

"Nice to meet you, ma'am."

"Did you call me ma'am?"

"Yes ma'am."

"You're such a sweet boy. And handsome too."

"Thank you, ma'am."

One of the first things they teach you in the streets is to respect kids and old people. If street boys find out you did some elderly wrong they'a beat you over it. And if you get sent up state having don' wrong to the old or young, they make you a jail bitch. All the boys in the ghetto know that's true.

When we entered the kitchen, his sister was standing at the stove. She was just as beautiful as the first time I saw her. I watched her. She was wearing shorts and this thin shirt with these thin straps kissing her shoulders. She was all skin, beautiful dark cinnamon skin beaming all kinds of browns and reds, like a pot of Mama's baked beans. Even her sandals seemed like they were in love with her feet. Her hair was in this haircut so when she moved her head her hair graced her neck and shoulders. She was a natural black woman and I was in love. She turned like she knew I was watching. She smiled.

"Hi," I said nervously.

She smiled bigger.

"I'm JuJu, Ashley's friend."

Her smile never left her.

"What's your name?"

"Naomi. Why?"

"Huh?"

"Why you want to know my name?"

"I don't know. I just do."

"If you don't know why, why you ask?"

Ashley tried to take some food. It looked like a TV dinner.

"This is Gran'ma's. Yours upstairs," she told him.

He headed to the back staircase. I wanted to talk to Naomi. I was just lingering. I didn't know what to say.

"C'mon man," Ashley called.

"Bye, Naomi."

I don't know why I said bye. It was the first thing that came to mind. I felt stupid. As we headed up, Naomi said, "Bye, JuJu." I couldn't tell if she was messing with me, if she was laughing at me.

We got upstairs.

"Man, yo sister is fine."

"Shut up."

"She is man, for real."

"Shut up. She can hear you."

I heard Naomi say, "It's done, Gran'ma."

"Told you."

In the upstairs kitchen, there was a dirty-looking pot with several hotdogs floating in it.

"What happened to the fries?" Ashley said.

Naomi yelled, "Peel some."

Ashley sucked his teeth.

"I told you I was making it," she yelled. "You act like you ain't want it."

He let out a breath like he wanted to choke her. "You want a hotdog?" he asked me.

"Nah."

"You can get one."

"I ain't hungry. I just ate."

"What y'all have?"

"Huh?"

"What y'all eat?"

"Oh, that was earlier."

"Okay, but what was it?"

"Pancakes, sausages, and eggs."

I could see Ashley was dejected.

"Oh," he said.

Mama was always making big breakfasts like that when one of her friends came over.

Ashley got his hotdogs and we sat on their ragged couch. The entire place was lined in dark wall paneling. They had this small TV on a stand that looked like one of them cheap metal TV dinner tables.

"Yo?"

"Huh?"

"How old is yo sister?"

"Shut up."

"I'm saying doe, what she like, sixteen?"

"Eighteen. Almost nineteen."

"Word?"

"Yeah. Now don't ask me about her no more or I'ma kick yo ass."

I thought he was joking. I thought he was gon' smile, but he didn't.

A door opened and Marquis came out of the only bedroom up there. He and Ashley share it. "Would you tell this idiot you can't stop doing something with cold turkey? He think because that commercial said you could stop *cold turkey*, that means you have to eat cold turkey."

"No I don't."

"Yes you do, dummy."

Ashley got angry. "I got company. Go back in the room."

Marquis sat in a chair. "It just mean you walk away from something, right?"

"Yeah. You just stop doing it without nobody help."

"I ain't never say you had to eat cold turkey."

"Yes, you did."

"Shut up before I punch you in the face. I ain't never say that. I was just playing with you. I should punch you in the face for eating all the fries."

"I ain't eat all the fries. Mama was here and she had some."

"Oh."

Ashley looked at me as he finished his third hotdog.

"Yo, you wanna play the game?" he asked, talking about *Super Mario Bros.*

"I ain't got no money."

"You don't need no money."

"Alright, c'mon."

"I'm coming," Marquis said.

"No, you ain't," Ashley shot back.

I gave Marquis a high-five as we left. "Next time."

When we got to Webbers, it was empty, aside from a few old ladies doing laundry. Ashley stepped up to *Super Mario Bros.* I thought he had some slugs he was trying to hide. He pulled on the joystick. The panel holding the arcade game together came apart and I could see exposed wires. Ashley reached inside and tapped this red button six times. It gave us six lives. He pushed the joystick back into place.

"See?"

We played *Super Mario Bros* for hours. Ashley gave us lives as we needed them. Neither of us were as good as Kevin. When I died, Ashley shook his head. "Man you suck."

While I was on the game a group of five entered Webbers. Tone was their leader. I heard the smallest say, "It's our turn, pussy." When I turned to see him, it was Raymond, a kid I knew.

"Yo, what up Rayray?"

He looked at me blankly. He let out a breath like I wasn't nothin'. Like he was mad I noticed him.

I've known Rayray since he was four. He transferred out of the Montessori school because he kept getting into fights. When he beat up this white boy real bad, they made him leave the school.

Tone said, "Fuck you looking at, *Ashley*?" He said *Ashley* like it was meant for a girl.

"Man, bump you," Ashley said.

Tone got in his face. "What?"

Ashley pushed him.

Ashley was a little taller.

Tone was a little older.

Tone said, "I should beat yo ass for puttin' yo hands on me. You lucky I don't fight little kids."

His crew laughed. They got between Tone and Ashley like he'd have to go through them first.

Ashley didn't back down. "Little? You talk a good game. You all mouth."

Tone said, "Yeah, like yo mother."

They laughed.

Ashley was upset. "What? Man, fuck you. Fuck you. I'a beat yo bitch ass in here."

I got off *Super Mario Bros*. One of Tone's flunkies stepped in front of me. I don't know him. He was looking me right in my eye.

"Over a game? Man, bump this game."

"Nah. Fuck that. What's up?" Ashley said.

Earl said, "Listen to yo boy *Ashley* before Tone beat yo ass."

"He ain't gon' do a goddamn thing ta me. I ain't scared of his punk ass. That's you."

Earl ain't say nothing. He just smiled.

In the ghetto everyone lives off reputation, or perception of their reputation. That's what gets you through. How people feel about you. If they think you tough. If they think you crazy. They'a only leave you alone if there's something to fear, or respect. They don't care if you smart. They don't care if you compassionate. They care if you a fighter. If you come from a lot of brothers. You have to have a reputation. You have to be known. Like Morris. People don't fight Morris, because they know he knocked people out.

I knew we had to let Tone win, for the sake of his reputation. I was trying to figure out how we could all walk away with our heads high. It was difficult because Tone disrespected Ashley's mother and that deserved an ass whoopin', even if she a prostitute. People talk a lot of shit in the ghetto, but one thing everyone agrees on is that talking about someone's mama deserves a beating.

"Yo man, we ain't trying to fight y'all over no game."

Earl said, "Shut the fuck up wit yo bitch ass."

"We gave y'all the game. Y'all starting shit for nothin'. Think we gon' just let y'all jump us and shit? We ain't stupid."

He stepped toward me. He was heavier than me. I was barely taller. Ashley stepped in front of me. He was just nodding like he was gon' kick my ass. Tone pulled him away.

An overweight black woman looked on. "Y'all stop that shit," she said. I went and opened the door. Old lady gave me a nod like I was doing the right thing. They wasn't gon' fight. They wanted the game. We backed out the door.

Tone couldn't leave it alone, he said, "Better run."

"Run? I'm right here." Ashley threw his arms in the air. "I'm right here. I ain't runnin' from nobody. One on one. What up? Bring yo bitch ass out here. Bet you don't bring yo bitch ass out here."

They all came out before Tone. Tone followed like he was some boxing great, relishing his limelight. Tone gave a flinch like he was gonna throw a punch. He never released it. On reflex, Ashley stepped back and swept his right hand like he would block the punch, and sidestep it. Ashley was on his toes.

Tone smiled. "G'on home, *Ashley*." Tone turned his back to Ashley and walked into Webbers.

"Turn yo back on me?"

One of the biggest slights in the ghetto is to be unbothered by a perceived threat. Ashley took it personal. Tone walked inside. His boys followed.

"I knew you was a bitch," Ashley yelled.

Tone had the game and that's what mattered. While we were walking away, Ashley was still angry.

"Bump them."

"Man, you know they ain't gon' give us the one on one. They just waitin' ta jump somebody."

"I know. When he by his-self, he don't say shit. Bitch ass. And he old as hell trying to fight us and shit. If I was seventeen, I'a be playin' these bitches. No what I'm sayin'?"

"Word."

13

We made it home. The night went by fast. We spent most of the afternoon on Ashley's stoop. Me, Ashley, and Kevin. Ashley was real proud I stood up to Tone's boys.

He said, "Thanks for havin' my back, man."

We slapped hands.

Kevin said, "Wish I was there."

Ashley was showing me their secret handshake.

"Not even Chill know it," he said. He kept saying, "Like this, like this."

After I learned their handshake, Ashley was telling me "the rules." Well, three rules. He said, "If you gon' hang with us, you gotta know three things. Number one, never speak out of turn."

"What that mean?"

"See. Let me finish. *Never speak out of turn.* That means never speaking on anything that don't concern you. That means never talking about things that has the possibility to make you a witness. Forget everything, like it never happened. No matter what they say, it wasn't us. Even if it was us. It wasn't us." Ashley and Kevin said that last "it wasn't us" at the same time. "You understand?"

"Yeah."

"Number two. People always talking shit. Like Tone."

Kevin said, "Bump that coward."

"Right," Ashley said.

They slapped hands.

"Number two. We brothers. You run. You my enemy. You his enemy. *One fight, we all fight.* That's rule number two."

"What's rule number three?"

"Don't get caught." They laughed.

When Ashley and Kevin finished laughing Ashley said, "Nah, seriously. Don't get caught. If you do get caught, that's on you. If one get caught, *he* get caught. You can't implicate nobody else. If you get caught, *you* did it. You. Not nobody else. Man up. No tears. Take that shit."

Kevin said, "Right. Be a man to the end. None of that weak shit. Can't trust no black man that cry."

They was both nodding. I was taking it all in.

Ashley said, "I should take my book bag to the Broadway Market. We should fill that bitch up, and hit the shortcuts."

We laughed.

"I'm serious."

"Cuz yo ass greedy," Kevin said.

Ashley smacked his teeth. He gave me a *Kevin is stupid* look, like I would take his side. I felt brave when I was around them.

"I'm down," I said. "Shid, let's do it."

Ashley was just nodding like we had a connection. "See, that's what I'm talkin' 'bout."

We laughed.

They was telling me I was one of them now. They kept saying, "We boys. We boys." I was smiling. I belonged.

It's funny. You think you don't want to belong, but you do. Everybody wants to be liked. Everybody wants to be respected. Belonging in the ghetto is like being indoctrinated. It's like how them cops build that border around the ghetto, but instead boys in the ghetto build a border around your mind. They make you believe and do things you shouldn't. Even if you know better. Even if you know it's wrong. Most people in the ghetto know they doing wrong. They know when they going for bad. It's just hard to fight it. Especially if they respect you. That's when you know you made it. When you respected. There's nothin' higher in the ghetto than being respected.

Chill came across and looked me square in my eye. "You in my spot," he said. "Sit down there."

Ashley and Kevin laughed.

Ashley mocked, "Yeah. Sit down there."

Chill got mad. I was his focus. "Get out my seat."

I made some room.

"Sit right here."

I didn't see the big deal. Besides, I was here first. Everyone in the ghetto knows, possession is nine tenths of the law. You learn that early. You learn that as soon as you old enough to take what you want. If you catch someone riding yo bike, they say, "It's mine now." You not even supposed to call the cops, if it was yo bike they was riding. Most people in the ghetto don't call the cops. Mostly because of the fear of losing your reputation. Also, for fear of police brutality or aggression. You supposed to fight them and win it back. A lot of people think if you call the cops that mean you a punk, or a snitch. Some people think calling the police on another black man is the lowest offense. That kind of thing messes with your reputation. Some people think it's wrong to sic the cops on other black people because they'a arrest you for anything, "just so they can get you in the system." Simple disputes always turn into street justice. If you lose something, it's lost. They'a say, "They ain't stop making these when you bought it." Even if you know it's yours, alls you can do is fight for it.

Some people write their name on everything. Still, it don't matter. One time Sean wrote his name on the inside of his right sneaker. This fat dude stole his sneakers from the PAL Center on Jefferson Avenue. When my brothers confronted him, he'd already marked lines with permanent marker over Sean's name. He also made the same permanent marker line on the left shoe. When Morris, Terrence, and Sean was gon' fight him he said, "I always do this—watch." He showed them another pair of sneakers with the same permanent marker inside. He said, "That's how I know they mines."

Terrence, who is the biggest at six-foot-two, 220 pounds said, "You probably stole those, too."

Sean said, "Yep, and crossed out somebody name."

Morris said, "Fuck that. Take his shit off."

I guess dude ain't want to get jumped so he gave Sean's sneakers back.

I went back to talking to Ashley and Kevin. "What'chu was sayin'?" I ignored Chill, like he wasn't even there. I was treating him like he wasn't even a threat.

Ashley raised his eyebrows like I disrespected Chill. When I looked at Chill, he smacked me.

He trying to play me, I thought. *He trying to push me to the bottom.*

I stood. My fists were tight. I lived by the rule Sean and Morris taught me. *Say whatever you want, just don't touch me.* I ain't no big fighter, but in the ghetto, you have to at least give an effort or they'll make yo life miserable.

They'a fight you every day if you don't stand up for yourself. They'a just keep pickin' with you until you stand up for yourself. Until you fight back.

Chill said, "What?" He did a fake flinch, like I was a bitch. I wasn't scared. I really wasn't. I ain't jump from his flinch.

I got off the stoop. He tried to smack me again, but I dodged and slapped him.

"Ooohhh," they said. Ashley and Kevin was laughing real big.

Chill was mad. "See, I was just playin' wit'chu." He got a mean look on his face. "Alright," he said.

It was a stupid reason to fight. I wanted to say something they teach you in the Montessori school or something I learned about perspective. How I wasn't trying to be disrespectful. How there's enough room. I knew if I did though, they'd lose respect for me. They'd say I was a pussy if I gave in and moved. I had to fight him. From the time he pressed me for the seat I knew I had to. I knew I had to let him know I wasn't gon' be the bottom dude everyone walks on. I could tell he thought he was respected more than me because he was friends with them longer. I could tell he wanted to have one of them "screw the new dude" relationships. I had to stand up for myself. Plus, you can't just let another dude slap you like you a bitch. You just can't. There's rules against that shit.

We started fighting. He was fat and slow, and his punches kept missing. I kept swinging. I musta hit him twenty thousand times. Ashley and Kevin was critiquing the entire thing. They was impressed with me.

"Keep swinging. Keep swinging!"

Chill hit me a couple time, but I was getting off more punches. He hit me one time in the stomach and hurried to drive me to the ground. I couldn't stop him from taking me down. He was on top of me. He hit me a couple times while I was on my back. I tried, but I couldn't do nothin'. I blocked. I dodged. He was slapping me real good. I hit him in the gut. It musta hurt him cuz he started holding my arms instead of hitting me.

Ashley stopped it. "That's enough." He dragged Chill off me. "Get yo big ass…"

I was still mad. I had my fist balled up, tight. "Fat bitch."

"Bump you." He gave me the finger.

I was mad. I wanted to kill his fat ass. He kept doing smacking motions with his hands, showing how he smacked me when I was on my back. He was mocking me.

Ashley put his arm around my shoulder. I had a tight throat. I was mad as hell. I was so mad I was about to cry, but I didn't. I wanted to get a knife and kill him.

"You alright," Ashley said.

I wasn't alright. I nodded I was anyway.

"Y'all done. That's it. We boys."

Kevin said, "At least you ain't no pussy."

I was still mad.

Ashley said, "It's over."

14

At the end of the month most people in the ghetto be hungry, especially those on public assistance. Usually food stamps is enough to get them through three weeks. I could tell Ashley was hungry. I heard his stomach growling. He was rubbing his belly looking all sad. When it got close to noon, Ashley came out with a sandwich and a glass of red Kool-Aid. Kevin kept looking at Ashley's sandwich. "What's that?"

"Egg salad."

"Boy, that's egg and bread. That's eggs and mayonnaise."

We laughed.

"It is Egg Salad, ain't it Marquis?"

Marquis nodded as he too ate an egg sandwich.

Kevin was relentless. "Y'all had some eggs and some bread, y'all made egg sandwiches. Ain't no egg salad, fool."

"Shut up talking to me."

"You mad? Dawg, he mad."

Our laughter continued.

"I'ma kick yo ass when I'm finished, watch."

It's always like that at the end of the month. You eat whatever you can get yo hands on. It's always a woman with kids going door to door asking for an egg so she can make deviled eggs, or "egg salad," or a pan of cornbread for her kids. Old people always finding cans to recycle for five cents so they can cook a pot of beans or buy a can of tuna or sardines.

Sometimes yo friends be dead tired. You see them. They can't even move. That's when white people go around saying blacks is lazy. Really, most people be hungry. People be starving. They be too proud to say so but that's the way it is. Sometimes you know yo friends ain't eat in two or three days. Sometimes they ain't had nothing in almost a week. You see people eating bread and mayonnaise. Or bread and syrup. Or bread and hot sauce. If people lucky they have hotdogs or eggs or bologna.

When they used to give out that government cheese, sometimes you'd go in yo friend house and everyone in there be nibbling that cheese. Sometimes you come in they house and they all be sitting around stinking like all that cheese don't agree with them. Sometimes all yo friends gotta stay in the house because they got diarrhea because they starving or because they ate a stomach full of that free cheese.

Don't nobody on public assistance ever have food for an entire month. Sometimes you'd see boys cattle rustling, when they go in the meat department and put steaks under they clothes and walk out the supermarket. In the ghetto, if it ain't enough to eat boys would also go out snatching purses or committing a robbery or any crime that you can get away with.

It was even tough for us unless Mama had two or three jobs. If Mama had two or three jobs, we'd always have a pot of spaghetti and a loaf of bread reserved for the end of the month. If she didn't, she'd send me to the store with a couple of dollars and I'd get a sleeve of crackers and some lunchmeat for me and my sisters. Them Arabs always breaking up products that ain't supposed to be broken. They'a break a box of crackers into four individual items, even when they ain't supposed to. They'a break a dozen eggs into individual eggs.

Ashley ain't hardly have nothin' in his refrigerator since we moved over here. This morning, me, Ashley, and Kevin walked up to Bells Supermarket on Broadway, across from Lincoln Academy.

When we entered Bells, Kevin, couldn't stop laughing his stupid laugh. *Hehehehe. Hehehe. Hehe. Hehehehe.* Ashley was scared he was gon' give us up. He looked at him real mean. Kevin stopped laughing as much. We was walking around Bells putting all kind of groceries in a cart. We didn't have one nickel. After we filled up the cart we went and got what we really came for, fresh donuts. They told me they do this all the time. They said, "We ain't never been caught. It's easy. Watch." So, I went with them. They filled up an entire dozen of donuts. My hands was shaking as I watched. You not supposed to be looking around when you stealin'. So, I kept my eyes on the donut case. They was careful to get the jelly because it was our favorite. Jelly and cinnamon rolls big as my hand.

We walked up and down aisles, putting food back on shelves and sneaking bites of donut. At first, I was scared. Nobody came to stop us, so I took a bite. Then another. Before long I finished two donuts. Ashley and Kevin was on to three and four donuts. They was laughing and fighting they hand in the box for who was gon' get the next bite. I kept thinking we was gon' get caught. I kept looking for someone to come and push us in the back, where they take all the thieves.

When they was satisfied, we made it to the register with that cart.

Ashley looked through his pockets. Kevin said, "Mama gon' be mad if you forgot the money."

The white woman at the register smiled at me. I was scared as hell. My heart was beating real fast. I kept wiping my face hoping she ain't notice I ate them stolen donuts. I was thinking about running but Bells has a security guard at the front door.

Kevin was licking his lips. He had Jelly in a corner. I wiped the corner of my mouth so he'd see me. Kevin licked his corners and smiled real big, showing all his teeth to the cashier. She smiled back.

Ashley said, "I'll be right back. Y'all put this stuff on the counter."

Kevin said, "I ain't doing it."

I said, "Me either."

I followed Kevin, who followed Ashley. When we made it past the watchful security guard, we knew we was in the clear.

People always be hungry.

Yesterday the cops tried to use that against us. Yesterday the cops parked a Hostess truck right on the corner of Sycamore and Reed. They just left it there, open. It was full too. All the boys was circling around that truck like sharks. They was going in taking arms of snack cakes and running. We was watching. I wasn't that dumb. Kevin wanted to go but we stopped him. Ashley said, "It's too easy."

When this boy named Lawrence come out with an armful, a thousand police cars flooded the neighborhood. They was going in and pulling boys from their houses for taking them snack cakes. All the old people and parents was mad. They came out by the dozens yelling at the police.

Lawrence father said, "What kind of shit is that, to put food in front of starving people like that?"

An old man said, "That's entrapment."

Someone else said, "Y'all just can't wait to get our boys in jail. Let 'em grow up and be a man first."

The only black officer said, "Free will. He has the intent to steal. We did nothing wrong."

All the adults was shouting how bad it was they did that to poor ghetto boys. The police didn't care.

Lawrence's father said, "Y'all put this truck in the white community?"

The officers didn't answer.

He asked again, to the black officer. The black officer ignored him.

Another man said, "Of course they didn't. They don't treat white boys like criminals. They don't hatch schemes on white children. They don't see us like people. They see us like criminals. They sit around all day in they office, thinking of ways to arrest us. Cops supposed to intervene in crime, not create crime."

Cops got mad and drove off in their patrol cars and that Hostess truck.

15

The last couple of days in June was the same every day. We sat on the stoop talking, telling jokes, and playing around. One day Chill and Kevin kept arguing over wrestling. Everyone knows that wrestling isn't real.

Kevin was trying to prove wrestling wasn't fake. He said, "Let me show you."

Chill and Kevin started to wrestle. They was going at it pretty good. Kevin was trying to pin Chill and Chill kept trying not to be taken to the ground. They ended up in the middle of the street. Horns kept blowing as cars sped down Guilford.

Chill's grandmother, a large woman called Big Mama, came out on her porch. "Stop that wrestling in the middle of street."

Kevin didn't listen to her. He tripped Chill and they was back on the ground. Kevin got Chill in a figure four-leg lock.

Big Mama was out on her porch, screaming. She rented a broken-down one-and-a-half-story blue house, across the street from Ashley. Her porch was ragged. Her wooden steps lifted every time you stepped on them. Her grass was uncut all summer and whenever the wind picked up, trash blew around her bushes.

"Stop it. Stop that now."

I watched Big Mama more than their wrestling match. She had nappy white hair she usually kept hidden under a scarf, but not today. It was the only time I saw her without it. They was pointing and calling her nappy headed. I liked her nappy white hair. It made her look like a lion. Most black people ashamed of their nappy hair. It's sad because it's the most unique thing any human got, aside from them Asian eyes.

Ashley was laughing his silly laugh. "Big Mama head look like a sheep ass," he said. "It look like that shit you take out of a pillow." He was bent over laughing.

I thought she was a good character for my writing. I wrote in a notebook all the time, a lot of stuff about living in the ghetto. Sometimes I made my own characters based on the books Boo made me read. She read a lot of books and sometimes I read them too, so she'a have someone to talk to about them. I was reading *The Catcher in the Rye*, just before we moved. Boo read it already. She said she read it twice. It's alright, only I don't like books about rich people like Cather or that Gatsby book.

Chill's grandmother reminded me of Mammy Two Shoes, from *Tom and Jerry*. I wanted to capture an image of her in my mind. I started remembering her in detail. *House shoes. Flower dress. Kind, church eyes. Hair like wool.*

Kevin let Chill go, but only after he agreed that wrestling wasn't fake. When they got off the potholes, Chill wanted revenge. He tried to catch Kevin, ignoring Big Mama's call, but he wasn't gon' never catch him.

Ashley said, "You ain't gon' never catch him, Fat Albert. He too fast."

That's what we did all day, at night I wrote about it in my notebook. One time I musta forgot about it and I took my notebook with me when I came down to the stoop.

Chill said, "What's that?"

"Oh. Nothin'. Forgot I had it."

"Let me see?"

"Nah. It ain't nothin'."

They pretended like they was talking again and when he thought I wasn't ready, Kevin tried to grab it. While I was trying to defend my notebook from Chill, Ashley snatched it and started reading.

"*She was the prettiest girl I ever saw. Brown skin. Big brown eyes. Long, thick hair. I wish she was my girlfriend…*"

They laughed at me. I could tell Ashley knew I was talking about his sister. His brow wrinkled. "Fool think he gon' be a writer or some shit."

Kevin got it next and kept reading. "*I wish we never moved on Guilford. I don't like it here. Everybody angry. I can't talk to nobody, except maybe Boo.*"

Kevin said, "Boy got a diary."

They laughed.

When I tried to snatch my notebook, Kevin threw it. "Fuck this shit!" They laughed. I wanted to punch him in his face, but I was new, so I didn't. I kept hearing the rules in my head: *One fight, we all fight.* I didn't want to fight all of them.

I was mad. I kept making pictures in my mind of Kevin's ugly face. His yellow teeth. His bad haircut. He said he cut it himself. Ashley had the best haircut. He ain't even pay for it. Last week, Ashley, Kevin and I went to the barbershop on Sycamore and Reed. There was this pretty black lady in there cutting hair. We was her first customers. Ashley went and sat in her barbershop chair. He told her what he wanted.

"Like, low but still so I got my waves."

"So just like an edge up, and a little lower?"

"Yeah."

She cut him nice. When she finished, Ashley looked in her mirror. He looked at Kevin. "How this look? She messed me up, right?"

"No, I didn't. I did not," she said, shaking her head.

"She did, didn't she JuJu?"

I didn't know what to say. It looked like she did a good job. I ain't say nothing. I guess I froze.

"I ain't payin'. Bump that."

She was looking all mad. "You gon' pay me something."

"I ain't paying you shit."

"What you say, boy?"

"I said I ain't paying you shit fo no messed up cut. Let's get out of here."

She was mad. What she gon' do, fight us? She ain't do nothin'. We left.

When we got in the street Ashley was mad at me. "When I ask you if she messed up, say yes, idiot. Closed mouth don't get fed. I'ma get mine."

Kevin's haircut wasn't nothing like Ashley's. Kevin's was messed up. He had what we call a one-two, in the ghetto. It was a bowl cut with no fade or nothing. It was just hair and skin, no transition.

I couldn't stop tightening my jaw, looking at his stupid face and his stupid haircut.

He stood erect. "What? Do somethin'."

People always think you have choices. They think it's easy to come from the ghetto and not be affected by ghetto people. Well it's not. It gets to you. It gets under your skin. Ghetto people can be unkind. They lack awareness of other people, and empathy. They tell you, "Fuck feelings. Do it!" They tell you to bury who you are. Get the job done. You must be reactionary and impulsive like them, or they don't like you. They have a way they want to live and if you won't accept it, they get mad. They ostracize you. Sometimes that's just the way it is. It's just the way the ghetto works.

I ain't fight Kevin, but I was thinking about it. Morris used to tell me, "Never let them rank you at the bottom because the dude at bottom gets stepped on." The days went by fast, and I got over it. I got over it. But I was mad.

16

On Independence Day, Mama made me go to a barbeque at her new boyfriend Corey's house. I didn't want to go to her new boyfriend's barbeque, but Mama was mad at me so I ain't have no choice. I don't like her new boyfriend. There's something off about him. He always trying to make me agree with him. "If only I could convince you, yo sisters would fall in line," Corey said to me. I don't accept most of what he believes. Besides, when Mama ain't paying attention, I catch him looking at Boo's developing breast.

Corey is a short black man with a nasty deep voice. He's the blackest man I ever seen. He so black even his fingertips are black. He has these nasty black lips. When he talk, even his gums are black. Even the whites of his eyes seem dark.

Since my father left, Mama only had two boyfriends I liked, Elijah and Sammy. Sammy was nice. He took me to see *E.T. the Extra-Terrestrial*, just me and him. It was the first time I ever saw a man cry. I thought he was cool so I ain't think nothin' about him cryin'. He wasn't never trying to con me or get in good with me so he could be with Mama. He was just himself and that was new for me. He ain't never walk like nobody or talk like nobody or use slang he heard somewhere. He was just a normal man and it was cool being around him.

This new guy is an asshole. Ever since they started dating Mama been acting real slick. She ain't been coming home from work. She stay gone for three or four days in a row, like when Elijah was looking for her. I ain't like him. A couple days back, we was riding in Mama's Ford Maverick and Corey told Mama he wanted a beer. He expected Mama to give him the money. She didn't. He was angry.

"What good is you?"

"I don't have no money."

"Well shid, I got these stamps."

Mama hates food stamps. Well she did, until she met Corey. Now, they ain't so bad. Mama used to hate people who spend food stamps, and people who live in housing projects. She cussed Sean out one time because he told her about his friend Booney, who moved in the projects.

Mama said, "Now Booney's mama know better than that. His mama ain't got nothing wrong with her ass. She need to get a gotdamn job. Don't be telling me about living in no gotdamn projects. I'a rather live in my gotdamn car."

"It's cheap, Mama. They ain't got no big light bill or nothin'. They ain't even got no gas bill at all."

"Boy, get yo ass away from me. I don't want to hear about it gotdamnit."

Sean was always hangin' out with them dudes who dropped out of high school. It used to be a bunch of them roller skating, partying. When Mama was at work and he was supposed to be watchin' us he'd lock us in a bedroom and have all kinds of girls over. They'd be getting drunk and smoking weed. Everybody liked him because he had one of them personalities like a famous person. He was real cool. All the girls was always trying to be with him. They was saying he looked like Bobby Brown. When he was younger Mama thought he was gon' be famous because he was always singing and dancing in front of the TV.

One time when I went to the bathroom while he was having a house party, I seen him in bed with two girls. He saw me looking. He just got out of bed and closed the door while he laughed. If Mama came home and caught him, she'd get mad and kick everybody out. She'd be cursing Sean to "get a job or get out." He left for a while but even them mothers in the projects didn't want him laying around partying and having sex in they house. When he came back home, he got the job in the skating rink.

Before she met Corey, if Mama saw somebody spending food stamps, she'd turn her lip up. Especially if she saw a man spending food stamps. That was the lowest. When they let Morris out of prison, he was with a girl who tried to get him on food stamps. Mama said, "Yo black ass bet not shine my doorstep if you do." Now Mama was all into food stamps.

"You can't buy beer with no food stamps."

"Why can't I? Pull in here."

We pulled into Wilson Farms. Corey turned around in his seat so he was looking at me and my sisters.

"Now I got these stamps." He tore one out of this book of food stamps. "A dollar each."

I sat there. It was the first time I'd ever seen a food stamp. Mama always said she'd rather be hungry than get food stamps—and we was hungry, too. We went without eating many times because Mama was too proud.

Mama looked at me in the rearview mirror. "Do it for me?"

I reluctantly agreed. Without my approval, my sisters wouldn't participate.

When we got in the store, it was empty. Corey turned to me. "See, ain't nobody you know in here." He had a big black smile.

A round white woman at the register welcomed us. "How you folks doing?"

I hesitated. I knew she was gonna be trouble. Mama always had trouble with white people who greet us with the word "folks."

"G'on now, get what you want."

I walked past the cashier. Corey stood at the end of her aisle, waiting. He gave her his polite, fake "nigger smile." That's what Mama called it. He was showing all his teeth like he was gon' be judged a bad black if he didn't make her feel at ease. It was something Mama must'a learned in rural Alabama, back when she grew up with them colored drinking fountains. It wasn't something I practiced, or cared for. I just do what I came to do. Get what I came to get.

Kimerlee grabbed my arm, ending my preoccupation with Corey and the cashier. "We can get whatever we want?" Her eyes were big.

Before I could answer her delight, Corey's voice shot down, "As long as it cost less than fifty cents." I could see he was calculating in his head and on his fingers. "Less than forty cents," he corrected. "Get a candy bar and come on outta here."

We found our treats. I got a Snickers. My sisters were in line in front of me, like I was told they must be, so I could watch over them.

The cashier gave a quizzical look. I could see her physically change, like she became someone else. The smile on her little round face changed into anger. I saw her, but she waited, making sure she was correct in her judgment.

When Kimerlee paid, Corey was there at the end of the line with his hand out ready to receive her change. The cashier's face got angry red. I mean, she was levels of red reserved for my principal at the Montessori school. I was waiting for their blowup as the cashier gave Terah change. After Corey received Terah's change the cashier refused to wait on Boo.

"No. You can't do that."

Corey got angry. "She payin' for what she got in her hand and yo job is to let her pay for it."

"No. I will not wait on any more of your children. Give me some of that change for these two."

"Do your job and stop worrying about what I got in my hand." Corey counted his change again. His face transformed. "Get your manager."

"No…I am the manager."

Corey looked at Boo. "Boo, pay for your shit. Give her the food stamp."

The cashier wouldn't take it. "Pay with that change in your hand."

"I want the manager, right now. Who are you to tell them they can't buy food with food stamps. Manager?"

The cashier said, "I am the manager."

"You ain't no manager. You just run the teller and think you got the right to tell me how to run my life. Do your job and give me my change."

"Pay with that change in your hand or leave my store."

"This ain't your store, you probably make a dollar an hour."

"Yeah well, I don't get food stamps."

"Good for you. You white. I get food stamps and whatever else I can get. I'ma get y'all for all y'all worth, like y'all did my people."

"Bullshit."

"What'd you know? Y'all keep pretending like what happened to my people ain't have nothing to do with y'all when half the politicians on

Capitol Hill voted for segregation. Shit, half the white people alive today voted for segregation. How you gon' say you had nothing to do with it, when you voted for the shit?"

"I didn't vote for anything."

"Well yo mama did, or yo daddy, or yo gran'mama or yo gran'daddy. Don't get mad at us for the seed you planted."

She rolled her eyes.

While we were waiting for her to take our food stamp, the store filled with customers.

"Y'all wait right there."

When it was apparent a line was growing behind us, the cashier got anxious. She tried to take someone in front of Boo.

"She's next. Him too. Don't let them skip in front of you, JuJu."

The cashier held firm in not accepting any more food stamps from us. The line didn't move. People were frustrated. A skinny white man emerged from the back of the store.

"Are you her manager?"

He nodded. "I'm the manager."

"She won't let them pay."

"He's already got a dollar worth of quarters."

"It's none of her business what I do with my change. They buyin' food with food stamps, and her job is to ring it up."

The manager agreed with Corey and after we paid, I watched the look Corey gave the cashier. It was like he wanted to humiliate her so instead of leaving, he went and got a forty-ounce beer. He paid with his illicit change. After she rung him up, he gave her his best fake nigger smile. "Have a good day, ma'am."

When he entered the car, he was seething victory. "Stupid fat bitch can't stop me, shid. And the manager knew I was right. He knew that shit was wrong. She was doing that shit on purpose. We can't buy food with food stamps. Bitch is you crazy? Bitch dun lost her gotdamn mind."

He was always like that. Terah asked Mama, "What's segregation?"

Mama said, "It's when white people use the government to keep black people low down and white people way up high." She told us a story about her father. "One time he wanted what was owed to him, because he worked an entire year and was paid five cents. White men came around in pickup trucks, shooting through the walls and windows. God saved me because I hid behind the chimney." She said two of her brothers got hit with "buckshots." One in the head. She said, "It was a bad time to be black. White people was…just mean back then."

Corey said, "Them fuckers mean, right now."

We laughed.

Mama kept looking at us in the rearview. "It's better for y'all now. You can be whatever you wanna be, if you go to school. Black people is thriving now."

For Corey's Independence Day barbeque, he forced Mama to give him one hundred dollars, cash, for the food. We had just come from Camellia Meats, where he spent food stamps for his barbeque. While I was in back with my sisters, it started.

"I ain't got no goddamn kids," Corey said.

"Ain't nobody tell you to spend all yo stamps on no barbeque," Mama shot back.

"You don't want no goddamn barbeque?"

"Look, not in front of my kids."

"I don't give a fuck." He turned around looking at us. "Y'all don't want no barbeque?"

I was angry. I didn't like the way he talked to Mama. "No."

"I knew you was gon' say that. You don't like me anyway. I see the way you look at me like you think you can whup me. Like you think this is yo woman. This my goddamn woman. You got that? You think you can whup me? Huh? Well say somethin' motha fucka. C'mon. You think you can whup me?"

Mama looked pitiful in the rearview. I ground my teeth into the back of my head so I didn't say anything.

"Leave him alone," Mama snapped.

"Nah, he always looking at me like he wanna kick my ass. Fuck that." He reached out his finger and poked me in my forehead. I knocked his hand down. "Think you tough. I'a beat yo skinny ass. Don't you never forget that. I'a beat yo skinny ass."

I lost a tear.

Mama stopped the car. "Stop it. Here, take it." Mama took all the cash out her purse and tossed it in his lap. "Take it. Take my goddam rent money."

I turned my head out the window so I didn't have to watch. Boo put her hand on my forearm. I was biting down so hard I thought I'd break a tooth.

"I don't want yo rent money. I just want a hunna dolla's."

He took his one hundred dollars and returned the rest to Mama.

"Just enough for this meat, baby."

17

While Corey was barbequing, I sat on his back steps. His yard was packed with his family: cousins, sisters, friends, nieces and nephews, everyone he knew. They was playing music and spades. They was getting drunk. They was talking, and dancing and eating. They was having a good time.

I wasn't. I didn't want to be here. I kept my Walkman on so I didn't have to hear them. I didn't have my notebook because I stopped writing a week ago, after Ashley and Chill and Kevin found it. If I did write, it was in my bedroom at night, when I was alone.

Once when Corey went into his house, he walked past me on his steps. "You don't want no barbeque?" he said to me. "It's good'er than a motha fucka, boy. I be cooking my ass off."

"Nah, I ain't hungry."

"Suit yo'self. Shit."

Mama came over while he was inside. "You don't want nothing to eat?"

"Nah, I ain't hungry."

"Don't be like that."

"What? I ain't hungry."

"You is hungry. You just don't want to eat because he bought it."

"He ain't buy it, you did."

"Alright. Mind yo business."

"Whatever."

"What'chu want from me?"

"I wanna go home."

"Look at yo sisters, they havin', fun. Don't take that from them."

They was having fun too. I kept watching Boo smiling and playing with all his cousins. I was still mad. I wanted to cry but I didn't.

"They can have fun. Just let me go home."

"You gon' walk?"

"It's not that far."

"You don't want no chips or nothin'? Not even a pop?"

"No. I just wanna go home."

"Go. G'on home."

I stood to leave.

"Wait," Mama said.

"What?"

"You serious?"

"I wanna go home. And you let him put his hand on me."

"Jesus Christ. I knew you was gon' say that. What you want me to do?" I could see she was thinking real hard.

"Don't go tellin' Morris he hit you either."

"I ain't."

"I mean that shit."

She reached in her purse. "Here." She gave me five dollars.

I left. I walked down Adams Street and headed up Sycamore. I could smell barbeque everywhere. It was like everyone was barbequing. I stopped at the corner store on Sycamore and Herman and bought some Little Debbie snack cakes, a dollar bag of Doritos, two Slim Jims, two Chick-o-

Sticks, and a quart of Upstate Farms grape drink. When I passed Kevin's house his father was cooking on a small ragged grill and drinking Thunderbird.

"Aye. Where Kevin at?"

He pointed up to Ashley's.

When I looked, Ashley was leaning out the window.

"Yo, come up," Ashley said. "The door open."

When I got up the front steps, they had a table in the living room where they was playing Monopoly. Ashley, Naomi, and Marquis. I didn't see Kevin. Ashley looked at me.

"You playing?"

"Yeah."

Naomi pointed. "Get a chair."

When I came back with my chair, Naomi was going through my bag. "Can I have a cookie?"

"Oh, yeah, I forgot I bought those."

"Strawberry? Why you ain't get lemon?"

"They ain't have none."

She opened the pack.

"Y'all can have those."

She passed them around. I kept looking at her. She was half dressed because of the heat. She had on these tight shorts that showed all of her thigh. I put my chair next to hers. She smiled. "Okay. One more game, then I gotta go."

"Where you goin'?"

Ashley jumped in. "She going to some party wit that fake ass punk she know."

"Watch yo mouth. Gran'ma can hear you."

We started a new game. Kevin came out the bathroom. I noticed his face.

A couple of days ago, Kevin didn't go to his mother's house like he promised—instead we hung out at Webbers and stole candy from the Broadway Market. Later that night we took out trash and mopped the floor at Alphonso's. They gave us free pizza subs.

Kevin ended up going to his mother's house much later than he should have. When he knocked, his stepfather came out on the porch. "What the fuck you knockin' on my door this late at night for, huh?"

Kevin seemed shocked. "Mama?" he called.

"Yo mama ain't here. She at work. She had to work the night shift cuz yo black ass ain't come home like you told her you was."

"I forgot."

"Forgot? *Forgot* don't pay no rent. *Forgot* don't buy no food. *Forgot* don't put no clothes on yo back. I had to come home early fo yo black ass."

Kevin let out a sigh. "So, I can't come in?"

"What you gon' do is, you gon' straighten yo black ass up. You ain't a kid nomo. You a man. Ain't nobody gon' give you no breaks nomo."

"I'm thirteen."

"You almost fourteen. What? Two months? When I was fourteen, I was workin'. I ain't have no mama. My mama died when I was a baby. Shid, I been workin' since I was five years old. I picked cotton. I had a goddamn sack on my back heavier than I was."

Kevin turned to me and Ashley. "Yo. I'ma catch up wit y'all."

We was concerned for Kevin.

"You good?" Ashley said.

His stepfather looked at us with contempt. "Yeah he good. He gon' be good or I'ma whup his motha fuckin' ass."

"It's cool," Kevin said.

We left.

Now I was just looking at Kevin's beat-up face. His stepfather had beat him so bad his face was lumped. His eyes were black. He looked like he lost a match to Mike Tyson. He seemed defeated.

"What you looking at?"

I didn't know what to say. I looked away.

No one said much of anything. It was quiet.

Ashley broke the silence. "Man, bump that coward."

I said, "Word. Bump him."

"Man, you bigger than him, just kick his ass."

He had a lump in his throat. "I can't. If I kick his ass I ain't gon' never be able to see my mama again." A tear formed in his eye but didn't release.

I said, "She yo mother, she gon' understand. He can't be givin' you black eyes and shit."

Ashley was angry. "Bump that. Man, I'm telling you, whup his ass. He not even yo blood, man. Let's jump his bitch ass."

Kevin snapped, "Y'all don't know what y'all talkin' 'bout. She ain't gon' understand. She already chose him over my brother. Now he livin' in a foster home."

I asked, "Cuz yo Mama put him out?"

"Yeah, man. They got into it."

"And she sent him to a foster home?"

"She kicked him out. He was livin' on the streets. His school took him to CPS. He 'bout to be eighteen so he 'bout'ta come home. Said we was gon' get our own place when he get out."

"So, what'chu gon' do?"

"I don't know. Nothin'. Ain't nothin' I can do."

"What about yo pops?"

"Pops ain't gon' do shit wit his drunk ass."

His pops called him. "Boy, get yo ass out here and eat. Now, damnit."

Ashley was making fun of him. "Come eat this burnt-be-que, boy."

We laughed, even Kevin. His father had been drinking and burning barbeque since school ended.

"I'a be back after I eat."

18

After Kevin left we got back to Monopoly. I only owned two properties, Boardwalk and Park Place, with hotels. It was Naomi's turn. She rolled and landed on Boardwalk. She was bankrupt.

"Aww man," she said.

Marquis couldn't stop laughing.

Naomi kept counting her money like we'd forget she owed.

"Pay me."

She looked at me with her sad brown eyes. "Guess I'm bankrupt." She owned orange and had hotels on Baltic and Mediterranean. She had a thought. "Or—or, how about this? How about I give you a hug, and we're even?"

I smiled. "What?" My heart was pounding.

"I'll give you a hug and then I don't owe you," she said.

Ashley was mad. "Nah, you cheatin'."

I kept looking at her.

Marquis too had a wrinkled brow. "Nah, I'ma win. Quit cheatin'."

I couldn't help it. I wanted to hug her. "Okay."

She pointed a finger. "And, I don't owe you."

One of her nipples stood erect.

"I know."

Ashley got up from the table. "I quit."

He went in the kitchen. I heard him open their refrigerator. When Naomi got up, she had on the tightest shorts I'd ever seen. She pulled on them and wiggled her hips as she stood. Ashley walked past us toward the front staircase eating a ham sandwich.

"Stupid," he said.

Naomi had the prettiest eyes I ever seen. I wanted to hug her so bad. She started laughing. She wasn't gonna hug me at all.

"Nah. Why you playin'?" I asked.

"I gotta get dressed for this party. I'm sorry."

I was dumbfounded.

She walked away laughing.

Ashley went downstairs. I followed him.

"What about the game. Okay I won 'den," Marquis yelled.

"Yeah you won," I said.

Ashley was sitting on his stoop. I sat next to him. He pulled a cherry bomb out his pocket.

"Where you get that from?"

"Store."

"They don't sell them at no store, it's illegal."

"Yes, they do."

"What store?"

"On the corner. Watch."

We walked to the corner store on Sycamore and Guilford. Ashley looked at the Arabic dude behind the counter.

"My man wanna buy some."

"Go. Go," he said, with a heavy accent.

Ashley led me to the small dark room behind the coolers. Three Arabic men sat around a floor full of fireworks.

"What you want?"

"Uhhh."

"What money you got?"

"Two dollars?"

"Good. Give me money."

I gave him my money and he gave me a small paper bag full of fireworks. I had three packs of firecrackers. I had this wheel with a wick on the end of it. I had a cherry bomb, a pack of sparklers, and a book of matches.

When we got back to the stoop Marquis heard us lighting firecrackers. "Let me get some firecrackers."

I gave him a pack.

"I'ma light these when it get dark," he said joyously.

Kevin came out to join us. "Where y'all get them from?"

"Store," I said.

"Pops got a roman candle. Said he was gon' light it when it get dark."

Kevin lit what looked like a firecracker he got from a pack in his pocket. When he threw it, it went into a dizzying spin of colors. When it fizzled out Ashley got off the stoop.

"Watch this."

He went and got a pot from his backyard.

We got off the stoop. Ashley went into the middle of the street and lit his cherry bomb. He put it under the pot. We took cover behind the tree in front of Big Mama's house. When it exploded, the cherry bomb blew the pot high into the air, higher than the street lights.

After the pot landed a car pulled up. The driver, a black dude, was wearing sunglasses.

"Y'all know Naomi?"

"Yeah. She my sister."

"Oh, what's up?"

"Ain't shit up. What's up with you?"

Naomi came out looking prettier than I'd ever seen her. She had on the tightest white shorts I'd ever seen, and this white half-shirt with ruffles around the waist. I could see her belly button. A beach hat with a dark brown band around it was on her head, and she had matching brown sandals with one grip between her big toe. She put on her sunglasses. "Ashley?"

"What? I'on know this fool."

"Stop it. And don't leave gran'ma. Foots 'posed to bring y'all some plates."

I couldn't stop watching her walk toward his car. It was like she was a model showing off her summer collection. I was awestruck.

She got in. They pulled off.

I lit all my firecrackers. I even put my cherry bomb under Ashley's pot and watched it send the pot higher than the street lights. Ashley argued that his went higher.

Mama's Ford Maverick pulled up in front of Ashley's house and she blew the horn. Corey was in the passenger seat.

Mama leaned over and looked at me. "Get in."

As I was walking to her car, Ashley yelled, "Yo, let me get that."

I threw him my paper bag of fireworks. Corey got out and I got in back with my sisters.

When Mama turned on Niagara, traffic going into LaSalle Park was crowded to a standstill. Corey had a bright idea.

"We ain't gon' never get in the waterfront like this. Turn over here. White people always trying to keep us from our shit when they want to use it. Man, you don't never see no white people around here unless it's the Fourth."

Mama turned and even the side street was packed.

"Go down this street."

"I'm trying."

"Turn, damnit."

I saw Mama looking at us in the rearview mirror. She turned down another side street.

"Now park right here."

"I can't park there. I'a get a ticket."

"You ain't go get no damn ticket, it's the Fourth."

We pulled into parking for one of the apartment complexes. Corey got out excited. "C'mon this way." He led us to a bridge that emptied into LaSalle Park.

When we got on the bridge it was nearly empty. Before we got halfway over the bridge it filled up in front of us. A throng of black people tried to get into the park but something was stopping us. When we turned to leave, there were more people behind us. We were trapped in the middle of the bridge. There was so many people the bridge started to sway. Everybody was scared talking about the bridge was gon' collapse.

Kimerlee started crying. "I'm crushed, Mama."

"What'a you want me to do?"

Corey picked her up and put her on his shoulders. Mama was happy. She gave him a kiss.

"What'a you see?"

"A lot of people."

He laughed. "I know, but what they doing?"

"They pushin' a police truck."

"The police done blocked us from the park," Corey said. "Ain't that a bitch. White people don't even like LaSalle Park, unless it's the Fourth."

Strangers pushed in front to get off the bridge and they pushed behind to get in the park. The fireworks started, so did crying from almost every kid on the bridge. People started cursing.

A woman said, "Hey, don't touch me."

A man returned, "Bitch, I ain't go to touch yo ass. Fuck you want me to go. We packed like sardines on this motha fucka."

Mama said, "You ain't got to be callin' her no bitch."

A girl not much older than me said, "This ain't the time nor place to be trying to cop no feel."

Her friends laughed.

I got over on the other side of the guardrail. There was a space without people pushing. The fireworks continued.

Boo pointed. "Look." She was standing next to me on the other side of the guardrail, looking at the fireworks. She looked dead tired.

While the fireworks exploded, officers came and escorted everyone off the bridge. They never let us in LaSalle Park. They never let us enjoy Independence Day.

19

After the Fourth, we was on the stoop chillin'—me, Ashley, and Kevin. Marquis came out on the stoop with us. We talked mostly about school. About our teachers. Teachers we ain't like.

Teachers in ghetto schools are the same as police officers. They be acting like they supposed to corral you, like they supposed to keep you in yo place. Like you a wild animal when you ain't. They be trying to act all tough and call you curse words when nobody looking. They be trying to challenge you to fights and make you look stupid in front of the class. Then they get all nice when yo mama come to school. That's what my teachers did to me. If they woulda just acted like I was alive and normal I woulda probably been they best student. But, I ain't like them and they ain't like me.

Marquis said something about missing school. Ashley frowned. "Boy, shut up. You sound real stupid. You think they like you? They don't like you. Listen. Last week, after we took the finals, I almost missed the bus because I forgot my hat. I ran to get it. The bus driver said, 'You got thirty seconds.' I ran in the building. When I got in there, I heard all these teachers laughing. When I got closer my science teacher, Mr. Pettipiece, said, 'And this poor bastard don't know Africa from South America.' I swung opened the door and Mr. Pettipiece was standing on a table, reading bad answers. They was sitting around him in a half circle, laughing. They were laughing so good they ain't even see me for a second. When Mr.

Pettipiece did see me they stopped laughing. I looked at their red faces. They had this look in their eyes like I had invaded some sacred space not meant for students. I saw they didn't really care about us like they said they did. They thought we was some dumb niggers. Mr. Pettipiece tried to get me in trouble. I ain't care. I ain't even listen to him. I ran to the bus. It's the last day—they can't do nothin' to me anyway. They don't like us. They pretend they do but they don't. They be trying to make you talk funny and say look'd'ed. They think it's real funny. They think we some charity that's gon' get them in white Heaven."

Marquis said, "School is fun. Being home all the time is boring. Plus, I wish I could get lunch."

Ashley smacked his teeth. "Free lunch start next week."

"They not gon' have pizza or taco salad or hamburgers or nothin'. It's just cold sandwiches and hard fruit every day."

Kevin said, "They do have pizza."

"Cold bread with cheese on it ain't pizza."

Naomi came and stood at the screen door. She always did that if we were making too much noise or if their gran'ma was trying to sleep. She was just standing there looking all sexy.

We got quiet. She leaned out the door.

"Marquis, Gran'ma want you."

"For what?"

"Change the channel."

"You coulda changed the channel when you came out here."

"I ain't want to."

"God."

Marquis huffed his way inside while Naomi got the mail.

We talked about going to play *Super Mario Bros.* Ashley's gran'ma called him. Her voice was stronger than I'd ever heard it. Ashley pretended like he didn't hear her.

"Ashley! Get yo ass in here. Right now," she yelled.

Ashley sucked his teeth and went inside. "I'a be back."

"Why you so smart at home and so dumb in school?" we heard his gran'ma ask him.

"I don't know," he answered.

"You do know, goddamnit."

Me and Kevin laughed. "Goddamnit," Kevin repeated, mocking the way she said it. We was laughing our asses off.

"You want people to think you dumb? I know you ain't dumb," his gran'ma said inside.

"I don't want people to think I'm dumb," Ashley said.

"Yes, you do too. You want people to think you dumb so you can do whatever you wanna do. You's a black man, Ashley. If you don't get no education, yo life's gon' be harder than anyone in this country."

"I know."

"Nah, you don't know, either. You don't know shit. You talk like you know then you go and get these grades. How come yo brother get A's and you don't get but one C?"

"Cuz, they don't treat him like they treat me…yet."

"Oh, goddamnit Ashley, that's it. I want you in this house. I don't want you runnin' them streets. I want you in this house for the whole goddamn summer. You hear me? Go read them books Naomi got from the library."

Ashley smacked his teeth.

"Goddamnit Ashley, I mean it."

"I'm not stayin' in the house for the whole summer, Gran'ma. I'm not."

"Then you can't stay here. G'on out there with yo mama. G'on and find her. She out there in a hole somewhere."

Ashley huffed to the door.

"I mean it, Ashley!" she yelled.

"I heard you!" he yelled back. To us he said, "Yo, I can't come out. Y'all comin' in."

As we stood to go in, Kevin Sr. came from between the houses huffin' and puffin'. "Boy you's a dumb summamuhbitch." Kevin Sr. threw a balled-up report card in Kevin's face. "Boy, get yo dumb ass in this goddamn house. You ain't going to high school next year?"

When Kevin got off the stoop Kevin Sr. pushed him to the ground.

"If they tell me you ain't going to high school I'ma beat yo funky ass."

Kevin looked scared as he looked up at his pops from the ground. "I gotta go to summer school."

"You been out here runnin' these streets and all the time you know'ed you wasn't going to high school?"

"I am going to high school."

"No, you ain't. Get yo ass in the house."

Ashley was laughing and pointing. Kevin was mad. I was laughing too. Kevin kept making his mean face like he was gon' fight us when his father let him come back out. His father kicked him in the ass.

Ashley laughed so hard his gran'ma said, "Boy get yo dumb ass 'way from that door."

When we went in, Ashley's grand'ma looked at me with mean eyes.

"Hi ma'am."

"Don't be ma'amin' me, goddamnit."

My eyes got big.

"They making it so y'all 'posed to be thriving, not failing. Dr. King probably rolling in his grave at you bastards. God rest his soul. I swear it ain't a black man between ya."

Upstairs, I could tell Ashley wasn't taking it well.

"Yo. Yo gran'ma trippin'," I told him.

He smacked his teeth. "I ain't stayin' in the house for the whole summer, I don't care what she say."

Naomi came up the back stairs eating an apple. "You gon' listen to Gran'ma or they gon' take you and Marquis away from me."

"I'm not stayin' in the house the whole summer."

"Ashley, you want them to put Marquis in foster care? You know how hard it was just to keep us together. Gran'ma only want us to be our best, that's all."

"I don't care. She don't know white people like I know white people. They always blame me. Someone else get in trouble, they come and blame me. They be tryin'a act like I'm the one when most of them dudes in school be stealin' from their purses and scratchin' dents in they car. I don't do nothin' and they always blame me."

"Ashley, I know it's hard for you but Marquis look up to you. You the only man he know."

"He don't look up to me. He think I'm dumb."

Naomi let out a breath.

Marquis came upstairs and turned on the television. He sat on the couch. It got quiet.

I looked at Marquis. "What you watchin'?"

"It's all messed up."

When I looked, it was fuzzy. "You gotta put a hanger in it."

"A hanger?" Naomi asked.

"Yeah like a coat hanger."

She went and got one. I bent it into rabbit ears and slid it on the back. The picture got clear until I took my hand off the hanger.

Ashley laughed. "That don't work. I tried it already."

"Here, hold it."

"No. It don't work."

"It do work. You gotta put a sock on it."

They laughed at me.

"A *sock*?" Naomi said.

"Yeah a sock. Like a boy sock."

"Ashley, get him a sock."

"No."

She smacked her teeth. "Marquis?"

"I ain't got no sock."

She went and got one of her socks. I was supposed to be thinking about fixing her TV but all I could do is smell the scent coming off her sock. I don't know what was wrong with me but all I could do was think, *I'm touching the sock she put her foot in.* My heart was beating so fast. It was like I couldn't catch my breath. I kept staring at the sock in my hand.

When I looked up, they was just looking at me like I was crazy. I put Naomi's sock on the hanger and put it back on the TV.

Marquis smiled. "It's clear. It's real clear."

Naomi looked at the screen. She turned the channels. "How you learn that?"

"Elijah showed me."

After a while Marquis took a dollar out of his pocket. "Go to the store with me?"

Ashley's brow wrinkled. "Who gave you that?"

"Gran'ma. For my report card. Said she gon' give me a dollar for every A I got next month."

Ashley smacked his teeth.

Marquis looked at me. "You comin'?"

Naomi came out the hall closet at the front of the apartment. "Can you go with him?"

We started out the door.

Ashley yelled, "Get me some Doritos."

Marquis laughed. "Nope."

"Give him fifty cent, Marquis. I'll give it back to you."

"No."

"Wait, I got some change in my purse." She gave me seventy-five cents for Ashley. Seven dimes and a nickel.

"What'chu want?"

"Doritos and some lemon cookies."

We went to Webbers because they always have lemon cookies, and when we came back Naomi was dressed to go out. I forgot I had Ashley's lemon cookies and Doritos in my bag. I was preoccupied by Naomi's glistening. She walked past me smelling so good, I wanted to inhale her.

"Did you get him his cookies?"

"Oh. Yeah. You leavin'?" I said nervously. It's the only thing I could think to say.

"I'll be back."

"Where you goin'?"

Ashley answered for her as I gave him his cookies. "She got some whack ass boyfriend."

My heart dropped.

"He not my boyfriend," Naomi shot back.

"Yes, he is. Y'all having sex, right?"

"What?"

"*What*, what?" Ashley grinned.

"Ashley, stop it."

"What? JuJu don't care, he a virgin anyway."

"No, I ain't," I said.

"You is. You probably never kissed a girl."

"Could you stop please?" When I looked at Naomi our eyes connected.

"Anyway, so are you," Ashley said to Naomi.

"How you know?"

"What'chu mean how I know. I raised you, that's how I know." Ashley smacked his teeth.

"You only four years older than me," Naomi said. "Anyway, could you please stop?"

"What? Marquis know anyway. Don't you Marquis?"

"What? That she goin' ta have sex with Billy?" Marquis said.

Naomi got angry. "Listen, stop it."

While Naomi was waiting for her boyfriend, Mama's voice broke through from downstairs. "JuJu? JuJu, get yo black ass out here right now."

Ashley was laughing, "Uh oh," he said.

"Shut up, fool." I got real brave. "I'a be right back."

Mama called again.

Ashley said, "No you won't."

They was laughing at me.

When I got downstairs Mama grabbed me by the collar. She was mad. I looked back and saw Ashley leaning out the window laughing and pointing.

***

When we finally got inside, Mama was standing in the living room with pain on her face.

Morris was sitting on the couch. "Hey, JuJu."

"What's up, Morris?"

He pointed at Mama.

Mama looked at me with her *I'm going to beat yo ass* face.

"What I do, Mama?"

"You know exactly what you did."

"What?"

"Yo teacher called Mama and said you called her a bitch. Said they was holding you back and you gon' be in the eighth grade again."

"I didn't call her nothin', Mama. She lyin'."

"Swear to God?"

Mama was always making us swear to God. She said God would get us if we didn't tell the truth. She said we'd go to Hell if we didn't. We all believed we'd go to Hell too, even Mama.

"I swear to God I ain't call her no B-word."

"Yes, you did. That white woman ain't lyin' on you."

"She lying, Mama."

"Well I think you lying. I think you done sold yo soul to the devil."

"What that mean?"

"It means you agreed to do all the bad you can, for the rest of yo life."

"I don't even like no devil, Mama. I ain't call her no B-word. I swear I didn't." I was lying to Mama but I begged God to forgive me. "Mama, I called her a dog. I ain't call her no B-word." I told God I wasn't lying because a bitch is a female dog.

Mama wasn't convinced. "Look at this." She put my report card right in my face. "You ain't pass not one class. They made me come all the way up there in the summer just to tell me how bad yo ass is."

I didn't know what to say.

"It say right here, you gon' be in eighth grade again."

"No, I ain't. You gotta take me to summer school."

She sighed. "I don't know what happened to you, JuJu."

"They make everything my fault, Mama. They try to get me in trouble and say I'm bad when the rest of them kids badder than me. They don't like me no more. Ever since I got on the third floor, they been tryin'na say I'm bad, and I ain't. Even before they find out who done somethin' they come right to me and say I did it, when I ain't even do it."

"I don't believe you. Them white people ain't tryin' to do nothin' but teach you how to learn."

"No, they ain't. They don't like me. Not one of 'em. When I was on the second floor, they all liked me. Now that I'm bigger, they don't like me no more. They pretend like they like me when you come to school but when you ain't there they treat me bad."

Morris said, "See, cuz you tall, white people scared of you."

Mama gave a humph, but the pain on her face lessened. She was thinking about beating me before he said it—I could tell because when Mama was gon' beat one of us she'd say we was evil and had the devil in us.

She said, "Somethin' ain't right and I don't know what it is."

Morris was still on my side. "See, you gotta smile at white people. You gotta show them you ain't thinking about no crime. They gon' always think you thinkin' about a crime, cuz you tall."

I was taller than Morris. Morris was five-foot-nine, but he was built like a tank.

"See, white people don't know what it's like to live in the ghetto and they think you 'posed to be walkin' around smilin' to show you good-natured. They don't understand you can't do that in the ghetto. When they see us lookin' mean they think it's cuz we mean, but it ain't. It's cuz we protectin' ourselves, from the ghetto. They think we supposed to be different in school than we is in the ghetto, but some people bring they ghetto life to school. Sometimes we gotta be the same in school as we is in the street, or they'a try to play us for chumps. We supposed to be learning, but we ain't. Then if you try to keep to yo'self they get mad and try to punk you because you won't belong to their group. And the teachers gon' always think you *black*. They gon' always make you prove you ain't. They gon' always think you trying to con them even when you ain't. The same with the system. The police gon' always think you know more than you do. They gon' always think you playin' a con game with them, even if you ain't. You gon' always have to give them all the good in yo life or they gon' try and blame you."

Mama was still angry. She looked like she ain't want to hear Morris' stories.

I did.

"Or the one time a dude in school said I tried to talk to his girl and so we had to fight. Now, neither one of us ain't fuckin' her—"

Mama said, "That's enough."

Morris stopped.

Mama said she was gon' take me to sign up for summer school. She said I better let them white people know I'm serious about my education.

"I told you I wanted to go to a different school. I told you they ain't like me no more."

"You staying right there with yo sisters. I need you to have yo black ass on that bus with them. You hear me?"

"Yeah."

"What?"

"Yes ma'am. Can I go?"

"You can take yo black ass upstairs. You ain't going outside no more. I want yo black ass in this house wit yo sisters, day and night. Night and day. And if they tell me you left this house, I'ma beat yo ass. You hear me?"

"Yeah."

"Don't be talking to me like that. I said, you hear me?"

"Ma, I heard you."

She was about to slap me.

"Yes, ma'am."

"You so gotdamn bad—and mannish, too. You think I don't know you be down there looking at that girl ass? Huh? You think I don't know that? You thinking I don't know you down there thinking about going to bed with her? Huh? You think I don't know you be down there trying to look at every womanly crease she got?"

Boo was smirking.

Morris was giving me a thumb's up. I tried not to smile.

"I see her with them shorts way up her ass so you can see everything the lord gave her." Mama turned to see Morris with his wide grin. "Don't be trying to corrupt my son."

Morris frowned. "Boys like girls, ain't nothing wrong with it."

"He a gotdamn child. Just cus you run around with everything with a tail."

"How this become about me? Let me get out of here."

Morris started out the front door. My sisters ran to him saying goodbye, giving him hugs. I sat on the couch.

"G'on and get away from me. G'on and take yo'self somewhere fo I change my mind and beat yo ass. I'm tired of yo shit. I'm tired of yo mood. You just like that motha fuckin' father of yours."

I knew she hated him. I knew she hated me cuz I looked like him.

I went and got a glass of water. Boo came in the kitchen. She put her hand on my shoulder while I was looking out the kitchen window, thinking about myself.

"You alright?"

"Yeah."

"Don't be mad at Mama, she just don't want her last son to be a failure."

"I ain't mad."

"You is. I can tell when you get mad."

"I ain't mad at Mama. I'm mad I ain't pass my classes."

"What happened?"

"I don't know. I'm just tired of everybody trying to tell me what to do all the time."

"If you gon' be smart you gotta be smart."

"What?"

"Well, you can't be smart and bad at the same time. If you gon' be smart you gotta be smart all the time."

"I just wanna be me. It just seem like being me ain't good enough. I don't wanna be smiling and jiving and coonin'. I just want to be me."

"Did you finish *The Catcher in the Rye*?"

"Most of it. I'm at the part where he tell that girl he wanna move away with her and she say no. When they ice skating."

"Oh yeah. It's good. I told you."

"What'chu reading?"

"*Huck Finn*."

"Did they say you can keep it?"

"Yeah."

"Maybe I'll read it after I finish *The Catcher in the Rye*."

I went to bed early, and just lay there thinking about myself. I didn't even eat when Mama called me to dinner.

"Eat, or don't eat. I don't care," she yelled through my door. "I know you mad…"

I put my headphones on.

20

This morning was the first time I been outside since Mama got mad about my report card. I woke up early and Mama drove me to Lincoln Academy on Broadway and Krupp Avenue, for summer school registration.

Lincoln Academy was a scary building for Mama. I could tell she didn't want to be here. When I was a kid my brothers got bussed to Lincoln Academy as part of Buffalo's desegregation strategy. On their first day, my brothers ran home because white people prevented them from riding the bus. I still remember when Morris burst through the door. Mama looked at him with a great fear in her eyes.

"What's wrong?"

"They chasin' us."

"Who? Y'all been fightin'?"

"Nah we ain't been fightin'. The kids ain't chasin' us, they parents is."

I musta been three years old. The thing about me is I never forget stuff like that. I never forgot that, or the time Sean came home looking like the elephant man. Mama asked if it was the parents who beat him

He said, "When I went to the bathroom them white boys just started beating me."

Mama was mad, but there wasn't nothin' she could do. They didn't believe him. They turned it around and said he went to the bathroom without a hall pass.

Mama said, "But that ain't no right to beat him."

They didn't care, they kept sayin' he wasn't supposed to be in there.

When he took a knife to school to protect himself, the white boys hurried and got the principal. They kicked him out of Lincoln Academy. Mama had to go to City Hall to get him in School 6, over there on South Division. It didn't matter. From that point on he ain't like principals or school or white people.

"They all working together to keep black people from making it," he said. "The police. The schools and the parents. They all working together so only them white kids get the good education."

We sat out front of Lincoln Academy while Mama collected herself. I could tell she was nervous. She looked at me. "Keep yo mouth shut. I don't want you to say shit. You hear me?"

When we got inside it was packed. All the parents had the same anger on their face. While we was waiting, I noticed this girl named Tasha from the Montessori school. She said, "Hi." I said hi back.

All the girls at the Montessori school have a dislike for me. Especially the black girls. They tell me I'm too black and too ugly for them. They say I don't walk with no limp and I ain't cool as the other boys. They even laugh at me because I don't play basketball. Her saying hi took me by surprise.

"Are you signing up for summer school?" she asked.

"Yeah."

"Me too," she said.

Mama grabbed my arm and pulled me to the desk. It was our turn. "This my son…" They went on with their introduction. Mama was nervous. White people always make her nervous. It's because Mama thinks all white people are important. I only get nervous around cops or if I'm in a business with a lot of white people. Or sometimes at school I get nervous when all them white people look at me like they judging me. I want to tell them I ain't thinking about no crime but I don't. One time when I was leaving the Buffalo Children's Hospital, I needed change for the bus. I went into one of the business on Elmwood. White people is always looking at you like you thinking about a crime when you come in their business so I said, "I just want change for the bus, I ain't no criminal."

This white teacher in front of Mama looked tired, like she was wasting her summer in this hot school. She told Mama how I couldn't go to summer school.

Mama was mad, mostly at me. "So, what you're saying is he ain't get no grades?"

"No. What they're saying is he's not ready and it doesn't matter what his grades are."

"I told you, Mama," I said. "How they gon' say my grades don't matter?"

Mama got mad. "Shut yo ass up."

The teacher continued with a smirk. "I'm telling you that's what his report card says. It says right here, ma'am, that he's not allowed to move into the next grade, so even if we took him in summer school, Montessori would keep him from being in the next grade. It would waste a seat for a kid who needs the seat."

Mama squeezed my arm when I turned to see if Tasha was listening. "So y'all won't even give him a chance?"

"It wouldn't make a difference. It's not up to us, ma'am. They're holding him back."

"I told you, Mama. They didn't even put no grades on there."

Mama tried to slap me. I blocked it with a flinch.

"Didn't I tell you? You gon' make me do something in front of these people I don't want to do."

She thanked the summer school teacher and we left. She wouldn't even let me say goodbye to Tasha. She pulled me to the door. As we exited, she said, "C'mon here, boy."

Mama dropped me off in front of the house.

"Keep yo ass in this house. If they tell me you was out this gotdamn house, I'm kick yo ass. I'm tired of yo shit. You need to straighten yo ass up, fo it's too late."

I went up on the porch. When Mama turned off Guilford, heading toward work, I went down to Ashley's house.

Naomi opened the door. "I think Ashley asleep," she said.

"Girl, you know I came to see you." I grinned.

She laughed. "You funny. Wait, I'll get him. Come in."

While I was waiting, their grandmother looked at me like she ain't like me. I didn't want to say anything to make her mad, so I just smiled.

"Can you turn my TV?"

"Yes ma'am."

I turned her TV to Channel 7, ABC. That's the channel all the old people watch because they like Irv Weinstein. If you know something smart all them old black people be saying, "Oh you a Irv Weinstein, or somethin'?""

"Thank you. That grandson of mine won't do nothin' I ask him to do."

"He just mad."

"Mad? I'm mad. You young people don't understand nothin' and got the nerve to be angry at something. Mad! Mad is when they tell you what you ain't gon' do cuz you black. *That's* mad. That's the problem—they let y'all do too much and y'all think that's freedom. That ain't no freedom. Freedom is when you become all that God said you was gon' be when he brought you into this world. You young people runnin' around doing nothin' and got the nerve to call that freedom. Become somebody important. Now that's freedom."

Ashley came down. "Sup?"

"Ashley, I don told you you ain't going nowhere, hear?"

"Gran'ma, we goin' to get a free lunch at the church."

"What church? St. Ann's?"

"Nah Gran'ma. The other church, right there by Fox Street."

She looked like she was thinking of the name, but couldn't remember it. I never remembered the name either even though we'd go there when we lived on Herman. All the kids would go there to get a hot breakfast in the summer. They was nice there too, especially the women. They'd watch us while Mama worked and we'd sleep on these rugs we had to buy from the D&K store on Broadway and Gibson.

"The red church, Gran'ma."

"Oh, you talkin' 'bout ole St. John's. That Lutheran church?" She nodded to herself. "They some good people. Sho' is."

It seemed like she was reliving a memory.

"Can we go?"

A minute later, Ashley came out on the stoop.

"Sup?"

"Shit. You know, report cards and shit," I said.

"They let you in summer school?" he asked me.

"Nah. You?"

"I ain't gotta go to summer school. I passed, I just got bad grades."

"Word? Yo gran'ma still trippin'? I thought you failed."

"Nah, she just want me to get A's," he said. "I got a bunch of D's, C minuses. But yo, I was 'bout to take Marquis to get a lunch, you comin'?"

"Yeah. Yo? What up with Kevin?"

"I been in da house. I ain't seen him. Knock on his door."

"C'mon."

I knocked. Ashley knocked. I knocked. Ashley knocked.

Kevin opened the door. "Sup?"

"Sup Kevin?"

He let out a sigh. "Shit. You know." His pops was home.

"Yeah. Me, Ashley and Marquis bout ta get a free lunch," I said. "You comin'?"

Kevin smacked his teeth. "Yo, come in for a minute."

We entered and was immediately in their dingy kitchen.

Kevin picked up a knife to continue cutting vegetables on a wooden kitchen table. "Hold on." He walked to his father's bedroom with the knife in hand. "Yo pops, can I get a free lunch?"

His father didn't answer.

"Pop? Yo pops?"

He still didn't answer. Kevin lifted the knife like Norman Bates. We laughed.

"You comin'?" Ashley asked.

"Let me get dressed right quick."

He put the knife on the kitchen table. He went to change. Kevin Sr. came out his bedroom.

"Fuck y'all doing in my house?"

"We waiting for Kevin. Me and Ashley…we was gon' get a free lunch."

"Kevin ain't going nowhere. Kevin, where you at?"

Kevin came into the kitchen with a long face. "We was gon' get a free lunch. I ain't wanna wake you up."

"Boy, didn't I tell you to cut them vegetables?"

"I did cut 'em, look."

When Kevin pointed, his father slapped him so hard it made his eye water. The kitchen reverberated with a sound I'll never forget.

"You take everything for a goddamned joke. Boy, I ain't got time fo yo dumb ass. Failing out of school. Kept behind like a goddamned retard. What the fuck wrong with you? When I tell yo stankin' ass to cut them motha fuckin' vegetables, you cut them motha fuckas. Where the onion at? Huh?"

Kevin was holding the side of his face. Ashley was laughing to himself and weighing down my shoulder as he leaned on me. I wasn't laughing. I watched as Kevin took the top off a bowl with cut onions, carrots, and potatoes inside. A stream of tears trailed from his left eye as it swelled. Then his right eye ran steadily.

"Y'all g'on on. Kevin ain't comin' outside."

When we were back on Ashley's stoop, I just couldn't understand it. I tried but I couldn't. I knew if I had a son, I'd never lift a finger on him.

When Marquis came out Ashley was still laughing.

"What'chu laughin' at?"

Ashley told how Kevin's father smacked him. He kept making a smacking sound with his mouth. He demonstrated on Marquis and they both laughed. My jaw was tight.

"It's not funny, man."

"I can laugh if I want to."

"Just saying, that shit ain't funny."

"It was funny ta me."

It never sat right with me. It reminded me of my father after Mama found out about his wife. His wife just showed up on our steps one day with her five kids. Mama stood there pregnant, looking at his family.

He wasn't never nice to us after that. He took it all out on us. If he was mad at Mama, he'd make us take cold showers or he'd put ice in the tub and make us take ice baths. He'd cuss us so bad my sisters would cry.

Eventually I stopped crying over it. He'd get mad that I didn't cry and he'd put me in a cold shower. He'd threaten to beat me with his belt because his cursing and cold showers didn't make me react, but he never did. I'd stand in the cold shower longer than he said I had to be in there. I thought, *If I act like I like it, he'll stop*. But he didn't.

For the rest of the time they was together, I had to watch him beat Mama. I didn't have a bedroom, so I slept on the couch in the living room. At night, I'd watch them come out of Mama's bedroom arguing. He kept saying Mama was "lookin' for somebody else." If Mama was winning the argument, he'd ball up his fist and knock her down. He even blackened her eyes one time because she got a drink at Stacy's Nightclub with this big black man from Texas. When they was fighting, I'd always pretend I was sleeping, but I wasn't. I was watching.

The last fight they had, Mama fought back. He kept saying, "Bitch, is you crazy?" When he was trying to hold her, Mama punched him in his head and he ain't like it. She threw Kimerlee's stroller at him, and he ducked. It broke the front window.

"Bitch, is you crazy?"

She threw lamps and candy bowls and anything she could. Several times she hit him. Then she ran off and came back with the biggest knife in the kitchen.

"Bitch, you crazy!"

He left. After that he never lived with us again.

I couldn't laugh at Kevin. I couldn't. Ashley could, and he did. Even as we waited for my sisters, Ashley continued to talk about Kevin's abuse like it was funny.

21

I returned to Ashley's stoop, despite my sisters threatening to tell Mama.

Kevin came out his yard.

"What's up man, you alright?" I asked.

"Yeah. It's whatever," Kevin said.

He ain't want to talk about his abuse at the hands of his father. He was looking off into space. Every now and again he'd play with his blackened eye.

Ashley came out. "Pops let you out?"

Kevin grinned. "You know he be having that drink in there."

"Yo pops be trippin', yo. The other day I was tryin'na sleep and I heard him and ole girl fightin' in the yard. Yo pops was like, 'You fucked him wit yo stankin' ass.'"

Ashley laughed. We all did. It was good to see Kevin laughing.

Ashley had an idea. "Yo? Y'all wanna go to Babcock?"

Babcock Boys' Center is in South Buffalo, a heavily Irish area—the Irish ghetto. Growing up, all the black people tell you the Irish got the most to lose, so they protect whiteness with their lives. I didn't know if I wanted to go. I remember dozens of stories of Irish boys chasing blacks home with golf clubs and baseball bats, just for walking through South Buffalo.

Before Mama got her Ford Maverick, she came home crying one day saying, "White boys followed me all the way to Broadway calling me nigger." She was in tears. It was all because she rode her bike though South Buffalo to get to work at the canning factory. "They just ran on the side of me saying nigger this and nigger that. Ugly nigger. Dirty nigger. Black nigger. They said, 'Don't ride though here, you fuckin' nigger.'"

My brothers wanted to do something about it, but Mama told them not to.

Morris was mad. "I'll walk up to anyone of them and knock his ass out for talking shit, Mama."

"I don't even know who they are."

"I don't care. Whichever one I see."

"I said no, damnit. Then you'd be just like them. They don't know me, that's why they call me a nigger."

Sean said, "It's about being black. They don't care about you. They don't care who you really are, so fuck 'em. Fuck 'em all."

Mama kept wiping tears. She was shaking. Morris had to bring her bike in the house. She kept hugging my sisters.

Boo said, "You ain't ugly, Mama. Don't cry. Jesus gon' get 'em Mama, watch. Treat a woman like that."

Mama said, "I been working hard all my life. I work day and night. I work two jobs. I don't never get to see my kids. I ride a bike ta get ta work. That's alright. God gon' work it out. They ain't gon' have no luck for that shit. Excuse me Lord, I ain't go'n say that while we talkin' yo good name."

Walking though South Buffalo is risky, but Ashley kept looking through the screen door, watching his gran'ma. When she was asleep, they convinced me.

Kevin and Ashley knew their way around Babcock Boys' Center. I followed them. We didn't play with any of the table games. I learned we were there to learn how to fight.

Ashley and Kevin went straight to the boxing equipment. When they was hitting the heavy bag, this old Irishman watched. He looked like that dude who trained Rocky. He came over just as I took a swing at the heavy bag.

"You boys boxers?"

Ashley smiled.

Kevin said, "Nope."

He looked at Kevin's blackened eye. He turned to me. "What about you?"

"No."

"That's a good hook you got. Won't hurt nobody, but you throw it well."

They laughed.

He started showing us pointers. He told me to use my speed because I was a "lightweight."

We stayed at Babcock Boys' Center longer than we should have, learning how to throw punches. When we were leaving, it was dark outside. I felt in my spine we were in trouble.

We started walking up Bailey, which was lit by more powerful streetlights. Even though I was fearful, not one white boy started any shit with us. We made it all the way to Bailey and Broadway, without any trouble.

When we started down Broadway, I felt a relief inside, knowing we'd made it. When I could see the sign that read *Memorial Drive*, I felt safe. Ashley was talking about being hungry. He said we should steal some candy from the gas station on the corner of Memorial and Broadway. When we started across Memorial, a little blue Ford Rabbit kept us on the curb. The passengers leaned out the window shouting, "Nigger, nigger, nigger!"

Ashley said, "Fuck you," and we gave them the finger.

As they turned onto Broadway, they leaned out the driver's side windows. "Nigger, nigger, nigger!" They had the biggest smiles on their faces.

In my memory, I created a picture of them, so I could write it in my notebook.

Ashley said, "Fuck you, you fuckin' hunkies," just like George Jefferson.

Mama said, "I never heard a black person say hunkie or cracker until Hollywood made George Jefferson say it." Mama was always talking about how George Jefferson was the most racist man on TV. How "it's a joke a black man is racist like that." She said, "I ain't never seen nobody be against so much the way they make George Jefferson be against everything. They think they slick. They making us the racists and all the white people angels."

The car turned down a side street.

"Fuckin' motha fuckin' dirty motha fuckas. Fuckin' devils!" Kevin shouted.

We was pissed.

When we got to Houghton Street, the little Rabbit shot out in front of us and stopped before we could cross. Five white boys emptied out of the blue Rabbit. They were all bigger than us and looked like them white boys from *The Warriors*, or S.E. Hinton's description of them greasers. They all had some object in their hand. A bat. A golf club. An industrial-size snow brush. A pipe. A tire iron.

The driver had this angular face I'll never forget. In my mind, I told myself he looked like *a feminine Batman.* I held that description, so I could write it later.

Batman said, "Who said it?"

My heart was pounding fear. How would we get out of this? I was thinking we should run, but couldn't say it because Ashley and Kevin would never respect me if I yelled, "Run." I'd be branded a pussy. So, I just stood there thinking about getting away and not being able to.

"Who said it?" he asked again.

Kevin said, "Who said what?"

"*Hunkie*, nigger. Who said it?"

Ashley said, "Who said nigger?"

"*I* did, nigger. Now which one of you niggers brave enough to say hunkie to our face?"

I said, "You think you can call us niggers, but we can't say nothin' back?"

"Fuck you, nigger."

I bit down on my back teeth. I didn't say anything. I kept looking Batman over.

He said, "Fuck you looking at, nigger?"

I sucked my teeth and let some air out my jaw.

"What nigger, you angry?"

I didn't say anything, but I never stopped staring.

He nodded to his boys, "Let's go. These niggers ain't brave enough. Fuckin' niggers."

They got in their blue Rabbit and drove off. We took off running. We didn't stop running until we were past Fillmore.

Ashley was mad. "They talk a lot of shit when it's a bunch of them. I bet not one of them would give us a one-on-one."

We walked home talking about what we would have done. Especially if there was only three of them. If we only had to fight one each, we'd kick their ass. If it was fair, if no one had a weapon, we'd kick some serious ass.

When I got home it was well past 11:00. I walked past Mama and Corey on the couch, watching Eddie Murphy on HBO in the living room. Mama didn't say nothin'.

I got in my bed and just lay there looking at the ceiling. I was too amped to sleep after dealing with them racists, so I started writing about it in my notebook.

22

We got up early to spend our Saturday playing *Super Mario Bros.* Nobody hardly plays on Saturday mornings, because everyone watches cartoons. I ain't hardly watch Saturday morning cartoons because my sisters would get mad if I tried to watch *G.I. Joe*, or *Spiderman and his Amazing Friends*, or *Transformers*, or *He-Man* or anything I liked. Even if I wanted to watch *Fraggle Rock*, they'd get mad. They'd cry to Mama and she'd come turn off the TV. "If y'all can't get along, can't nobody watch TV."

Me, Ashley, and Kevin figured we could play as long as we wanted, and no one would stop us from hoggin' the game. Earl and his boys would probably be sleeping or somethin'.

Well, it didn't happen like we hoped. After playing for almost two hours, Ashley was on the board everyone called "the Everlasting," because it kept repeating. Super Mario would run through the screen and come back to the beginning.

"No one makes a game that doesn't end," I said. "It's impossible."

"No one can clear the Everlasting," Kevin said. "That's why they call it the Everlasting, dummy."

I wasn't convinced. I'd stay in Webbers for hours, by myself, trying to solve the Everlasting, but I never could. I was convinced it was some kind of puzzle I just couldn't solve.

Tone and his boys came in—angry.

While Ashley was about to reach the Everlasting, Tone snatched him off the game. It seemed easy, like Ashley was a toy being thrown to the floor. I was taken by surprise. Ashley looked shocked as he lay on the floor.

Kevin shoved Tone. Earl got right in Kevin's face. A balding, Irish-looking dude started yelling at us to "Get out the store! Get out. Get out!"

Outside, it just started. Ashley was fighting Tone. Kevin was fighting Earl.

A punch connected with the side of my face. Tone's flunky was laughing. "Right in the jaw."

I was mad as hell. I was in a rage over being hit.

While he was laughing, I swung and hit him on the side of the head. The next punch was his and he hit me so hard I had a whistling in my ear. I was surprised I didn't fall.

I swung, throwing as many punches as I could, but compared to Tone's flunky, I was a lightweight. I was knocked right on my butt.

I looked around and everyone was bloody. Ashley and Tone was fighting to a standstill. Kevin was getting the best of Earl.

"Stay down," he said.

I spat some blood and felt a lump growing outside my jaw. I tightened my fist and hit him with my best hook.

He threw a wild punch. I ducked. I hit him three or four times as fast as I could. His brow wrinkled. I hit him again before he saw it coming.

He grabbed me around the waist and was on top of me. I could feel he was as tired as I was. I grabbed his arms, refusing to let go. I could barely hold him. I looked up, praying someone would stop him. I didn't see the blue sky this time. No, this time I saw a shoe coming down on my face.

I was out. Unconscious.

***

When I finally woke, Morris was standing over me. He kept slapping my face.

"Stop it," I tried to say. I tried to say it again and it came out, "Top it." I guess I had a swollen lip. Probably a concussion and who knows what else.

When I got home, Mama was mad. "Didn't I tell you to stay yo black ass in this house? Huh? Didn't I?" She pushed me down on the couch. "Out there getting yo ass whupped. I told you I ain't want you hanging with them bad ass motha fuckas no more, didn't I?"

She slapped me. She slapped me right where it was sore.

I looked at her real mean.

"Who you looking at like that, huh? I'ma beat yo ass cuz I den told you I ain't want you out there. It's bad enough you ain't gon' pass to the next grade. I should'a beat yo ass for that. Let alone fighting all in the street like some criminal."

I kept playing with a wilt on the side of my jaw.

Morris said, "He been hit enough, Mama."

"That's my child. Don't tell me how to raise my son. He ain't gon' be no criminal like you. They got yo bad ass in prison, looking all stupid. Then you wanna call me. Don't call me. Don't call me for shit when they get yo ass behind them bars. Make them fast-tail girls bring yo ass some Kool Aid."

"All I said was—"

Mama ain't want to hear nothing from nobody. "Get yo ass outta my house, right now. Ain't you got someplace place to be? Don't tell me shit. That's my son and he ain't gon' be no criminal."

"I'm yo son too."

"Yo ass is grown. I tried. Lord knows I tried to raise you right. You didn't wanna listen. This boy ain't but thirteen." She looked at me. "You sit yo ass right there on that couch and don't move. Cuz I'ma beat yo ass."

I was a lump of embarrassment.

Mama went to her bedroom and was still cussing me from there. "Dumb. Black. Motha Fucka. Stupid sonuva…ooohhh. Ooohhh. That burns my ass. Fighting out in the street like a wild dog. Who raised you? Oh, I'ma give you somethin' to fight. Just wait. Just wait. Ooohhh. Ooohhh. I'ma show you better than I can tell you. Just like that lyin' ass daddy of yours. I can't stand his ass neither. Lyin' all the gotdamn time. I'ma give yo ass somethin' to lie about in a minute."

Morris sat, probably thinking about all that Mama said to him. He stood. "Let me get outta here."

We slapped hands.

"Thanks."

He said, "You'a be alright," and slapped my shoulder.

He started out the door.

"Wait. Wait." My sisters ran to hug him. He left.

Mama came out her bedroom with a leather belt over her shoulder. "Stand yo ass right here."

I went and stood next to the wall. I was mad. My sisters looked on.

"Didn't I tell you?" She hit me with her leather belt. It was a good first flurry. I stood there unmoved. I didn't even flinch or nothing. You can't let on that it bothers you, that it hurts. Not in the ghetto. Not even with you mama. You can't let them break you. Not the police or white people. Not your friends or rivals. Not nobody. That's just the way it works.

"I told yo hardheaded ass." She swung her belt again. She got a real good swing on my arm, the third time around. I rubbed the pain. It was like she was happy about it. Like she had gotten through to me.

On her fourth go at it, I caught her belt.

Her face changed. I could see it—she was scared of me. I didn't want her to be scared of me. I just didn't want her to hit me anymore. It's a tough place to be in. Especially with my mama. I understood Mama been raised to believe you have to break a black boy. To break him and make him mind. It's typical. It goes back to slavery. Black boys have to be broken or they ain't no good. If you too brave or mannish it's because you ain't been whipped enough. Because you ain't been broken. It's like a part of the ghetto home training is to break you down to nothin' so you'll be good for white people. They'll even say it. "I'm doing this so white people won't have to." It's always like that. "Wait till them white people get hold of yo stupid ass."

They always trying to make you be a good black. Everybody wants to break you to their rule when you a black boy—the police, teachers, adults, white people, other black boys and even yo mama. If you ain't smiling and happy and dancing, everybody think you guilty. Even if you ain't. Even if you just quiet and you don't like talking or smiling. If you ain't no dancing happy black, they get intimidated for nothin'.

I could see in Mama's eyes she was afraid. She probably thought I'd take the belt from her and use it myself. They always think the worst outcome. They always think you thinking 'bout killin' them or somethin'. Even if you ain't. I wouldn't never hit my mama. I had so much respect for her. But I wasn't scared of her anymore. That fear she tried to raise in me left when I got taller than her.

I let her belt go. She was dumbfounded. She didn't know what to do. She was stuck. She looked real confused. She dropped the belt to her side.

"Go. Get out of my sight."

I went to my bedroom. I heard Mama laughing with my sisters, although I could tell it was out of fear and not humor. I didn't like it. I didn't know what to do with myself, after Mama beat me with her leather belt, so I started writing about growing up in the ghetto in my notebook.

I wrote an entire page that just said *fear* a thousand times. *Fear* and *black fear*.

23

This morning Mama told Ashley I couldn't come out. I heard him out there yelling, "Punishment." I wasn't even on punishment no more. Mama was just mad she worked a double shift yesterday and we ain't clean up her kitchen, after cooking all day. She was real mad.

"Why y'all gotta drink outta so many gotdamn cups? It's like thirty cups in the damn sink. Drink outta one damn cup. I'm tired of this shit. And who left these pots in my sink?"

Everybody said, "Not me."

That's when Mama got real mad. "One of y'all did it, damnit. It's only y'all. Ain't nobody else here. Who did it, the invisible man?"

No one would own up to it.

"That's it, gotdamnit. I want this motha fuckin' house clean or I'ma beat somebody ass. And think I'm playin'. And turn off all these gotdamn lights too, gotdamnit."

That's when Ashley banged on the door.

Mama said, "Don't be knocking like the police this early in the gotdamn morning. He ain't coming out gotdamnit." She slammed the door in Ashley face. Mama told me if I clean, I could go out. "For an hour," she said.

I cleaned the house with my sisters' help. I went over to the stoop after I finished. Marquis was playing out front with one of his friends.

"Yo, where Ashley?"

"Upstairs."

When I got up the front steps, I heard Naomi say, "Wait. I'm dressing." I stood there thinking about how she was probably naked on the other side of the door. My mind kept saying, *Burst in and look at her*, but I didn't. I waited. I waited and thought about her nakedness. My body kept reacting to my thoughts of how beautiful she was.

I looked at the ceiling and prayed I could think of something else before she saw me. When Naomi opened the door, delicious smells and her beauty hit me. *God, she is the greatest woman I ever seen.*

"What'chu doing today?" she asked. She turned and walked toward the kitchen. I watched her. I followed.

"I don't know."

She had the best butt I ever seen. Most black girls have nice butts but Naomi had the roundest, most shapely butt.

"Ashley? I'm finished," she said.

Ashley came out of his bedroom. "What up?"

We were sitting on Ashley's stoop—me, Ashley, Kevin, and Marquis. Kevin was talking about going to Alphonso's—Ashley was wondering if they'd give us a full pizza instead of pizza subs—but we ain't go because Naomi left and Ashley had to look after his gran'ma. We played Monopoly all night and I didn't go home until midnight.

Mama ain't say nothing. Matter of fact, I ain't even see her. She was in her bedroom with Corey. I couldn't sleep so I stayed up reading. I tried to write but I couldn't focus on nothin' but visions of Naomi.

***

The next day we just hung out all afternoon. Chill was at Big Mama house. She let us come in to play Atari. We played Donkey Kong for four hours. All of us—me, Chill, Ashley, Kevin, Ronron, and Dondon.

When the streetlights came on, a car started honking nonstop. Ashley looked out the window and laughed. We wanted to know what was so funny.

"Yo mama out here, Dondon."

"Quit playin'."

"I ain't playin'."

The horn kept blowing until Big Mama opened the curtain.

"That's yo mama."

Dondon and Ronron hurried off the plastic-covered blue carpet we'd been sitting on, passing around the joystick. They had this hurry about them as they started for the door.

Ashley said, "G'on home, Mama's boy."

Ronron said, "Bump you."

"Bump you too," Ashley replied.

Dondon crossed a line. "At least we got a mama."

"What? What, bitch?"

Big Mama said, "Alright now."

When I looked, I saw a picture of a shiny white Jesus behind her. Everyone knew she was a good church lady. She ain't like cussing. Even if adults cussed around her, they'd beg her pardon.

Ashley tried to follow the twins out the door. We stood in his way. Me and Kevin. We held him back.

"Fuck you bitch ass punks. G'on home to yo mama. Fo' I put my foot in yo ass."

In unison, Ronron and Dondon gave Ashley the finger.

"Y'all get out my house with all that cussin'. G'on 'head." She grabbed Chill's arm. "Not you."

"I can't go on the porch, Big Mama?"

"Not tonight."

While we walked off the porch, I watched the twins' car pull into their driveway. When I was about to cross the street Ashley and Kevin grabbed me. They didn't want to go home so we ran off Guilford.

We was just walking up Broadway looking for a good time. That's what I thought. When we got into the white neighborhood Ashley smiled. "Yo, you see that?" Four bikes were parked out front of Alphonso's pizzeria. All the white kids hang out at Alphonso's. Inside, as soon as you enter you see several arcade games. There's *Donkey Kong*, *Tetris*, *Asteroids*, and *Galaga*. Ashley got down lower than the window. He was like a cheetah or something, stalking. He looked back at us.

"C'mon."

His face was wrinkled like we was punks. Like we was scared. Kevin followed.

What if we get caught? I was thinking. *How we gon' get back to Guilford with stolen bikes? Is cops watching us? Is some hero white man watching?*

"Man up," Ashley said. My heart was pounding.

I'm not a thief, I thought.

"You down, or not?"

I nodded. I crept behind Kevin.

Ashley looked inside Alphonso's. "Sucka ass white boys. Like kids," he said.

Ashley pounced. He was on a bike riding toward Bailey before me and Kevin had a chance. Kevin was laughing his stupid laugh.

We was gone. We was riding toward Bailey. We couldn't go back toward Fillmore on these new bikes. We was gon' have to make a circle around the whole ghetto and sneak past the cops on side streets. We was laughin'. Kevin has the dumbest Scooby Doo laugh, I swear. His laugh was so infectious. For some reason I was laughing. I wanted to believe I was laughing at his laugh but I knew I wasn't. I was proud of myself. I didn't even know why.

When I tried to take my bike in the house, Mama stopped me. She slapped me right in the face.

"A gotdamn thief. That's what you are? You a gotdamn thief? Get that stolen shit out of my house right now. Don't be bringing no stolen shit to my house. They should do like the Bible and cut yo fuckin' hand off. Ooohhh I ain't know you was gon' be like this. I throw my hands up to you, Lord. A hard head make a soft ass. He don't listen to me no more, Lord. He don't. He yours Lord, do with him what you will."

Ashley was laughin' when I told him what Mama said.

He took me to the junkyard—we wasn't keeping them bikes. We sold them for twenty bucks each. Ashley went to Super Duper with his money and got hotdogs and bread and potatoes and something to drink. I bought a lot of junk food and shared it with my sisters while Mama was at work.

24

I couldn't stop hanging with Ashley and Kevin, even though Mama said I should. I just couldn't do it. I was having too much fun. She told me I was supposed to stay in the house, but I ain't listen. I couldn't. She ain't have no more threats except "Listen or let them white people teach you when they get you in they system." I wasn't gon' get in they system. I wasn't doing nothin' like she thought I was doing. I ain't no bad black boy. I was just hangin' out and enjoying my summer.

On July 16 Ashley turned fifteen. He ain't have no party or nothing. Ashley ain't get nothin' for his birthday, not even a cake. I ain't have big parties or get gifts on my birthday either, but Mama always got me a cake. Even if I ain't want it.

She'd buy me a cake and say, "Eat it anyway."

To be honest, I was always happy she bought it. Ashley ain't have a cake or chips or pop or nothin'. Whenever he went in the house, we was talking about doing something for his birthday. I had fifty cents. Kevin had a quarter, and the twins had a dollar. Chill was at his mother's house over there off Suffolk, in the Langfield housing projects. We kept talking about it behind Ashley's back.

Kevin said, "We gotta do somethin'. We brothers, man."

"What about cupcakes?" I said.

Kevin was laughin' about our birthday secret. Ashley came out.

"What's so funny?"

"Nothin'."

"I know y'all ain't laughing about me. What? I'ma be a fifteen-year-old freshman."

Kevin said, "Chill, man. We ain't laughing at you, dude."

Ashley had to go back in the house to talk to his other grandmother on the phone from New York City. We ran and brought Ashley three packs of cupcakes for his birthday. We was laughin' when he came back out.

"Why y'all laughin'?"

Kevin threw the bag of cupcakes at him.

"Happy birthday," we said.

You shoulda seen his smile. Man, that was the biggest smile I ever seen. We ain't have no fights or arguments or nothin' the whole day.

It's funny cuz Ashley and Sean got the same birthday: 7/16. That's they birthday. That's also Buffalo's area code.

The day after Ashley turned fifteen, Sean came home. I was happy to see him. We ain't even see him like we should. Mama said, "He made his choice. He know I got babies to think about." If we did see him it was like two or three times a year.

Everybody was happy to see him. Mama threw him a party and we was all out in the yard celebrating him. Everybody was there—all his friends, his girlfriend, everybody. Even Ashley and Kevin, was there eating grilled hotdogs. Everybody was having a good time. We was eating and they was drinking and talking about the cakes and balloons Mama brought Sean from Super Duper. One cake had *Welcome Home* written on it. The other said, *Happy Birthday, Sean.*

When everybody was having a good time, I noticed Sean was missing. He'd gone inside. I went to find him. He wasn't in the bathroom. When I got upstairs, he was sitting on my bed, reading my notebook. I just stood there unable to tell him to put it down. He looked up and smiled.

"You wrote this?"

"Yeah. It's just stuff."

"When I was in juvy I read that Lorraine Hansberry play. *A Raisin in the Sun*. You ever read that?"

"Nah."

"It's nice. You should read it. It's about how white people keep us from leaving the ghetto." He held up my notebook. "I like this. It's good."

"It's alright."

"Nah, I like it. Is this me right here?"

"Where?"

He pointed. "Right here. This dude. Willie. Is that me when we was in the snow that time?"

"Oh. Yeah."

"You really thought I was cool like that?"

I didn't say nothin'.

He was just nodding his head, looking at me, and back to my notebook. "I like this, it's really something. You good, boy." He smiled like he had a passing thought. "Yo?" He was smiling real big. "You still do them Kermit the Frog voices?"

"No. I can't do it no more."

"Why not?"

"My voice changed."

Sean laughed real big. "Growing up huh?"

"I guess."

"Yo, when I was in juvy there was this dude that used to beat-box just like Doug E. Fresh. Yo, that boy used to remind me of you though. I kept tellin' them cats can't nobody beat-box like you, man. For real. Yo, hit a beat for me."

"Nah man. Don't nobody beat-box no more."

"Word? That shit dead huh?"

We ain't talk for a minute.

"C'mere, come sit down."

I came and sat next to him.

"Yo. Look at me."

I did.

"Never let them put you in juvy. Never. Jail. None of that shit. Never let them take yo freedom."

"I'm not."

"I'm serious."

He put his arm around my shoulder. I sat there looking at the floor.

"Nobody should ever have to be locked up. People supposed to be free. Not locked up. Listen to me. Never stop trying to make it. Never let Mama look at you like she look at me. Like I ain't nothin'. Like I ain't gon' never be nothin'. Like she gotta worry about me all the time. I'ma grown ass man. You listenin'?"

"Yeah."

"Be somethin'. You can make it out of here, JuJu."

I didn't know if I could make it or not, but it helped that he thought I could.

He smirked. "I remember when yo ass was little. Now look at you." He pulled me closer, rocking me back and forth. "You like a little ass man now."

I'm taller than him, now. Sean is maybe five-foot-ten. When he went to juvy, I was shorter than him.

"I'm sad I missed all this, man. Really. I'm sad I missed you grow up." He put his hand on my thigh. "You gettin' some fuzz?"

He broke out laughing when I hesitated.

"Don't worry, they gon' give it to you. You tall. Girls like that."

Sean was always the flyest dude in the neighborhood. Everybody looked up to him. Everybody liked him. Especially the girls.

"Just be tall and keep yo shoes clean." He laughed. "I'm serious though. Girls like that." He got real excited. "Yo? Yo? When I was in juvy you know what I seen? I seen two birds fuckin'. Ain't that some shit?"

"Mama calling you."

He gave me my notebook. "Keep writing them stories, boy."

"I am."

He left me there holding my notebook.

25

When I came back the day after Ashley birthday, it was almost noon. Ashley was still sleeping. Marquis was laughing when I came over. "He got high and passed out. It was funny." Marquis kept showing me how Ashley "hit the joint and passed out, trying to out-smoke Mama." Apparently, his mother came home in the late night and smoked marijuana with Ashley.

When I got upstairs Ashley was a ball on the couch. He sat. "What's good?" I could hear Naomi running the shower. We sat there talking, me and Ashley. Marquis came and turned on the TV. After about ten minutes Naomi came out of the shower. She was wrapped in all kinds of towels and a housecoat.

"Good morning," I said.

"What time is it?"

"Almost noon."

"Why?"

"I think I got a job."

She walked past us to her queen-size bed in the living room. She was so beautiful. I watched her more than I watched their TV. Ashley was still high, I could tell. I couldn't stop thinking about Naomi. Naomi was different. She was a woman. A day didn't pass where I wasn't sitting on the stoop thinking about her. If we was out there and she was leaving, I'd get the sweetest smells of woman when she squeezed between us. I'd watch her walk until she was out of sight. She was always going for interviews and trying to get into training programs. She'd get mad because we'd leave the street.

"Goddamnit Ashley, I told you to stay with Gran'ma." She would be real frustrated. "Listen, we have to work together. I coulda been in college right now. If I can do it, you can do it. Stop acting like that. Gran'ma need all of us. You can't be leaving her with Marquis."

One time she came and found us. "Bring yo ass to the gotdamn house right now, Ashley." She was standing there with her fist tight. I was smiling. Watching and smiling. Ashley was trying to ignore her. She got mad.

"Now!"

"In a minute."

"Right now, gotdamnit."

Ashley laughed. "Girl, you don't scare me."

"What? See…"

She chased him. She was faster than Ashley, running and jiggling like a girl and I was watching, smiling. Fascinated.

Ashley kept sayin', "Alright. Alright. Damn."

"Don't cuss me, either."

Most of the time when I came over, she'd be at the kitchen table filling out applications. She said she wanted to go to college in Buffalo and in Georgia, but she was waiting "till Marquis finish grade school." She had it all planned out. She was going to college once he finished, "no matter what." She wanted to get a biology degree. She wanted to become a nurse. A lot of black women want to become nurses. You hear a lot of the older black women saying, "Don't be wiping no shit, like me. Don't wipe no ass. Be the RN."

She actually got accepted to college in Georgia, but she didn't go because Gran'ma got sick real bad. She had a stroke and one of her arms ain't work no more. One of her legs was too weak to stand without a cane or that metal walker.

Naomi coulda left. She coulda been free. I woulda left. I woulda got out of Buffalo, so I can be where people don't treat black boys like we a threat to them.

I would come in and ask her what she was doing. She ain't never roll her eyes or nothin'. Sometimes Ashley would push me if I watched her too hard. If I was trying to have a conversation with her, he'd say, "You ain't got no shot, fool."

Naomi would just smile. "Ashley?" she'd say, making him stop. Sometimes she'd tell me I was cute. I mean, if she needed something, she'd tell me how "cute" I was.

One time Ashley wouldn't go to Webbers to get her a bar of soap. She looked at me with those big brown eyes. She was really playing it up, all sad and puppy like.

"JuJu?" she cried.

I woulda done anything she asked. Anything. I couldn't wait for her to give me her money—maybe she'd touch my hand. I ran to Webbers and back in less than a minute. When I came back with her soap, she was upstairs. Ashley told me to "give it to her yo'self."

My heart was beating so bad as I made my way up the front steps.

When I got up there Naomi was sitting on her bed, her bare legs coming out of her house coat. She was just humming some song, bouncing her crossed leg on top of the other, filing her fingernails.

I took a breath. Her skin. My thoughts. She was glowing, radiant. She smiled. She opened her palm. I gave it to her. I was so nervous.

"Thank you. Wit yo cute self," she said. It was all sexy like she was trying to entice me. Her smile was so sweet. I wanted to pour my heart out to her. I wanted to tell her she was the prettiest girl in the world, but I didn't. I stood there looking at her longer than I should have.

She smiled. "Thank you."

I said, "Bye," and went downstairs with Ashley and the rest of them.

Today, Naomi went into the hall closet and came back out. "I have to change," she said.

Ashley and Marquis stood and turned their backs to her. I followed them. "Don't turn around," she said.

Something was happening to me. I couldn't help it. I turned my head. I had to see her. I got my eyes on her just as she dropped her housecoat. She wore a bra and panties. She was amazing. Her body was better than any woman Morris showed me in his *Playboy* magazines.

My heart was full of flutter—something was driving me to watch.

She took off her bra and wiped her hand over her perfect nipple like something was attached to it. When she put her hands on her panties I was fully engaged. She slid her panties down. She was neatly shaven and barely had hair except a neat little patch. When she rose from taking her panties off, her breasts bounced.

"Almost ready," she said.

I was dumbfounded. I was in love. I wanted to be her boyfriend.

Our eyes met. She quickly covered herself with her hands and arms and her brow wrinkled. She didn't say anything.

I smiled nervously.

She took her arm away to expose her breasts. I looked them over again. She pointed her index finger. I followed it to her eyes. She did a twirl with it, instructing me to turn my head away from her. I turned from her nakedness.

After a minute, she said, "Okay." Ashley and Marquis went back to sitting on the couch watching TV. Ashley was high or dizzy or something. He fell into the couch, his eyes still red from all that weed he smoked with his mother. I sat on the edge of the couch trying to hide my excitement. I could only think about her nakedness, about Naomi being naked right in front of me.

"I gotta go to the bathroom." I got up and rushed into their bathroom.

Something was wrong because I couldn't pee. After I got back to normal, I stood in the mirror looking at myself. My mind was racing. I kept seeing her naked body. I kept seeing her breast and her groomed vagina.

She knocked. "JuJu?"

"Yeah. Ahhh. I'm comin'. Hold on."

I opened the door. She had on a nervous smile. She put her finger over her lips asking me to keep our secret. "It's okay."

I nodded. My eyes never left the floor. She shook my shoulder. "You okay?"

"Yeah."

"Good. I'm okay too."

I stood there longer than I should have. She smiled politely. She was waiting for me to leave the bathroom. "Oh. Sorry."

I returned to my seat with her brothers. After a while Naomi left. I continued to talk with Ashley and Marquis until it got dark, but from time to time I'd see a vision of her nakedness, and I'd get excited. When my excitement finally subsided, I stood. "Yo I'm 'bout to go home."

***

When I was in my bed that night all I could think about was Naomi. I lay on my back with the most excitement I ever had, just throbbing as I thought about her naked body. I tried to read *The Catcher in the Rye*, but I couldn't think of nothin' except Naomi.

For the rest of the night, I listened to music on my Walkman. I just lay there thinking about her. I didn't even eat dinner.

"Eat, or don't eat. I don't care," Mama called. "I know you mad…"

I put my headphones back on. When I finally fell asleep, I dreamed I was with her.

In the morning, for the first time in my life, I was soiled.

26

The next day we was in Alphonso's taking out their trash and mopping their floors. We came lookin' for bikes but wasn't none out there. While Kevin was in back swinging the mop, a crew came in. One said, "Townsend, bitch."

What he was saying was, "We are Townsend, we fight as one." That's the way it works in Buffalo. We don't really have gangs. It was just, if boys on one street wanted protection in fights, they represent their street. It wasn't really about territory, it was about numbers.

Me and Ashley didn't say anything because they had us outnumbered. It was probably twenty of them.

One of them said, "Which one of you bitches wanna fight?" He was pointing like, *Eeny, meeny, miney, moe.*

Ashley said, "I ain't tryin'na fight all y'all. One on one?"

He took a swing at Ashley. Ashley ducked and pushed him back to his friends. While I was watching, another took a swing and grazed my chin as I pulled my head away. I was mad. Ashley grabbed me when I tried to swing back. Kevin was watching from the window in the service door. They started laughing with the one who grazed me.

He said, "I woulda knocked his bitch ass out."

Antonio, the owner's son, racked a shotgun and they took off running. I looked at Antonio not expecting him to save us like that. He nodded like he had our back.

While we were appreciating Antonio's victory, I heard a woman scream, "My purse. He snatched my purse!"

They let Kevin out the service area and gave us our food. We took off running. We ran behind the Broadway Market. We ran through the bank parking lot across Fillmore. We ran through all the backyard shortcuts I didn't know about yet. When we finished running, we were inside Webbers, eating our pizza subs. We was lucky we ain't get jumped. We was lucky none of the police caught us.

I kept thinking we shoulda made it home, but crossing a big street like Broadway only gets you noticed by all the sirens. At least that's what Ashley said. He was eating and laughing and sweating. I was listening to the sirens. My heart was pounding like they was after me.

They thought it was so funny. I didn't. I was on the lookout, barely eating, watching, listening for the sirens. They was sure we was lucky, until a car parked out front. I knew they was cops because when I was little, they parked out front of our house in the same kind of unmarked car.

Sean was sleeping when they knocked on the door.

"Hey, is your mom home?" they said when I opened the door.

"She's working."

"Hey buddy, can you open the screen?"

When I opened the screen, their faces changed, they pushed me to the floor and ran upstairs and got Sean out of bed, at gunpoint. They didn't care they made my sisters cry. They didn't even care we needed Sean to cook us lunch. They just left me there with my hungry sisters.

I said, "Yo. Cops man, cops!"

Right after I said it, Kevin looked.

"Damn man, don't look."

They came in. Two of them. Two tall white cops, in suits. We were the only ones in the laundry, so I knew they was coming for us. They just looked at us. I knew they was waiting for us to talk first. We didn't.

"Where'd you get the food?"

I said, "Store."

"Oh yeah, what store, wise guy?"

My heart was beating so fast I couldn't talk. It felt like the blood was beating backward in my heart. Felt like my heart was doing backflips.

Kevin said, "Alphonso's."

"Oh, you boys were up that way, huh?"

"We work there."

"You work there? What, you boys swinging dough?"

Ashley said, "We mop and take out the trash, and shit like that."

"And shit like that?" He looked us over. He looked under our chairs. "You boys don't snatch purses, do you?"

We were innocent, but I was scared. I just knew they was gon' beat us and take us to jail.

One time when I was little, they beat this dude half to death and left him in the dirt between the shortcut. We watched them do it. When we called the ambulance, people was out there telling the ambulance it was the cops who did it. So many people yelling at the ambulance workers that they called the police because they was scared. The ambulance people wouldn't even work on him until the cops came to protect them from all the screaming.

When everyone told who did it, the cops said we was lying. They got their boss out there and he promised he'd get to the bottom of it. He didn't though. Instead, he made them cuff the beaten man to the stretcher.

They said, "He hit a cop. He's being arrested for battery on a police officer."

People was saying, "I watched it. I watched it. He ain't even have no chance to hit no cops. They was beating him. I seen it. They had him on the ground. He was blocking like this. Naw, they ain't beat him with no sticks, they beat him with they fist. I seen them kick him. Kicked him good, too. Kick him right in his face."

Them two cops in suits was standing over us looking real mean. I was thinking they was gon' take us and beat us in a field somewhere. I knew they was gon' say we snatched purses.

Kevin said, "Nah, that ain't us."

"That ain't you? Then who is it?"

"I don't know man. I'm just sayin' that wasn't us."

"But you know it happened?"

"What?"

"You said it wasn't you like you knew it happened before I told you it happened."

I knew we was going to jail.

Ashley said, "You tryin' to pin it on us but we ain't do nothin' like that."

I said, "We didn't do it, Officer."

He just shook his head like I was lying. He pointed at me. "You was in Payless, right?" He smiled real big. He looked at our sneakers. He looked at his partner. "That's him, right?"

"Looks like him."

I took a deep breath.

"See, we know who you boys are. We know three boys who look just like you stole a bag of candy out the Broadway Market the other day."

The day before Ashley's birthday we went in the Broadway Market all bold. Ashley brought his book bag this time. We filled it up. When we was trying to leave the guards came out and chased us all the way home. The only reason we got away was because we hit a shortcut on Guilford, that took us to Herman, then we jumped a fence on Herman, and hid behind Mr. Andersen's garage.

Then the next day, Ashley's birthday, we stole beer and chips. It was the most fun I ever had. I was free. I was having fun. My face hurt because we was laughing so much. Now, officers were standing over us like we killed someone.

He said, "Which one of you boys did it?" He pointed at me. "I think it was you."

"No, it wasn't."

He looked at Kevin. "What about you?"

His partner said, "I think it was this one."

Ashley kept eating his sandwich. The officer asking all the questions got mad. Ashley took a bite when they asked if he did it. He smacked Ashley's sandwich to the floor.

"Damn man," Ashley said as he stood. Ashley was taller than him.

He pushed Ashley in his chest. "Sit down."

Ashley stood again. "I was gon' eat that."

The officer tried to push him in his chest again. Ashley knocked his hand down.

"Don't touch me. I ain't do nothin'. Threw my food on the floor. I was hungry. Why you do that for?"

Ashley looked at his sandwich like he was gon' pick it up off the floor and eat it anyway. The officer took Ashley to the ground. He had his arm around Ashley's neck.

"You blacks always gotta be tough, don't you?"

That's what they always say. It's like officers believe every black man is Muhammad Ali or Mike Tyson or something. They think we all tough. They be acting like they about to get credit for fighting a lion or something.

"Wanna be tough?" he said, as he choked Ashley.

I could see Ashley wasn't tough. I could see fear in his eyes. I don't think he ever thought he'd be the one on the ground being choked, but he was.

I stood. His partner got right in my face. I knew if I looked him in the eye it would be me on the floor being choked. That's how they want you. Broken. Afraid. Scared to state your rights.

That officer was choking the life out of Ashley. Ashley's eyes rolled in his head. I couldn't even say nothin'. I couldn't even help him. One fight, we all fight?

It looked like the officer was enjoying it, like he was wrestling a wild animal. It was like he was proud he'd defeated such a big black man.

Police. They want you to walk around with yo head down. They want you to pay them some deference. They want you to know, they'a break you.

Ashley couldn't fight his choke no more. He was lifeless. He stopped moving. I couldn't even tell if he was breathing.

The officer cuffed Ashley. Man, I was scared. I thought Ashley was dead.

He stood over Ashley looking mean. "C'mon. Stand up."

Ashley ain't move.

They cuffed me and Kevin. I ain't wanna be cuffed. I ain't fight it though. How could I?

Ashley still ain't move for a long time. I swear I thought he was dead. When they picked Ashley up, he was like a drunk. His legs wasn't moving right. His eyes was different. They was holding Ashley up by his belt.

I called him. "Ashe? Yo Ashe?"

He opened his eyes. He looked at me with a tight jaw. He groaned. He coughed. I was happy he wasn't dead.

27

When we got to the police station on Fillmore and Broadway, they kept calling us "the Guilford Street boys." They said we was part of a gang. We said we wasn't but they said we was. They took our fingerprints. They took pictures. I seen when one officer wrote under my picture that I was "affiliated with GSB." I had never even heard of GSB.

The whole thing was dehumanizing. Being cuffed. Getting printed. Takin' that gotdamn picture. Felt like they was cataloging us. Felt like someone had just shot an elephant and was tagging their kill and getting a picture so people would believe them when they said they shot it. It just felt wrong. Felt like I wasn't a person no more. Felt like I was some black they had been hunting. Felt they was gon' go, "See, this a nigger right here." Like they was gon' laugh and say, "We got one."

I kept thinking JuJu probably dead now. Now if they see me walking they'a get out and say, "What you doing, boy? Where you going, boy? Oh, I know you. I remember you. Ain't you GSB?" Then I would say, "No, I'm JuJu," and they'a start laughing. They'a start laughing cuz I wouldn't be JuJu no more. I'd be exactly what they thought I was. I'd be a bad black. Don't nobody care what they do with bad blacks. It feel like most white people don't even believe it's a sin to kill a bad black. If they killed me now they'a say he was a GSB. They'a make it so the good white people in this world wouldn't feel nothing about how I was killed like a dog in the street. They'a give them cops who killed me forgiveness. All the good white people with hearts about killing would say, "What was that cop supposed to do? The boy was GSB." They wouldn't even say I was JuJu. They would just tell themselves I deserved to die because I wasn't no good black.

It's the worst thing that could happen if you a black boy if the police know you, if the police get you in the system. Once that happen, you cooked. You an example. They can do whatever they want to do to you after that.

How could I be this stupid? Stupid enough to get arrested? I'm supposed to be smart. I'm supposed to be a writer. I thought about all them adults on Humboldt Parkway. I could hear them telling me I was smart. I thought about Mama and her jobs and how she always telling us she don't want us to mop floors or clean toilets.

I lost a tear. Ashley elbowed me, but I didn't care. It was too late. I kept hearing them say, *"You're smarter than that."* I kept hearing Mr. Williams say, *"Run with them and become them."*

Mr. Williams was smart. He was a cameraman for Channel 2 WGRZ. Before we moved off Humboldt Parkway, he'd pay me twenty bucks to cut his grass, a big empty lot next to his house. Everyone thought I was crazy for doing it. Sometimes it took me a weekend, but I never gave up. Henry used to do it, but he stopped because he said it was too much work. He was even laughing at me. It was a tough job. But how could I quit? Mr. Williams trusted me. He gave me the key to his shed. He even paid me half the money before I started. Maybe it was a test.

He told me, "Last time I gave Henry half the money up front, he didn't cut my grass. You ain't gone stiff me, are you?"

People in the ghetto are always trying to test you like that. Always trying to gauge your level of deceit. They assume you're trying to take advantage of them. Even in the working-class parts of the ghetto, they assume you're trying to stiff them. People in the ghetto have been beaten by so many scams, they don't trust anyone. It's like part of your upbringing is to distrust everyone.

I wasn't scamming Mr. Williams. In fact, when I looked out over his lot and saw his grass as high as my knee, it was like a challenge. I couldn't turn it down.

Mr. Williams would tell me I was a "good young man." He'd say, "That Henry's a con. He's just looking to be something he don't got to be. He got good parents. His mama almost a nurse and his daddy working at Dunlop. He don't gotta be out here cheating people. Stay away from him. He ain't good for you." I knew he was right too. It's easy to understand when they ain't good for you, but it's the hardest thing in the world to say no to their friendship.

When Henry was a junior in high school, he got this bundle of raffle tickets. He got a couple of us grade school boys together and we went around selling them. We sold them for twice of what we were supposed to.

People would say, "It say fifty cents on the ticket."

Henry trained us to say, "That's the price for supporting our class trip, but if you want to win that TV, you gotta pay a dollar."

Most people would pay the dollar too. They ain't even ask no questions about it. We made eighty dollars. Henry had to turn in half the money for his high school raffle, but he ain't care. He gave us a dollar each, leaving him thirty-five dollars. He was laughing his ass off. He said, "Next time, I'ma get a thousand tickets." Henry had a lot of scams like that. He was a real hustler. When one of the old ladies complained that she paid a dollar to win the TV, Henry got in trouble.

I kept thinking about what Mr. Williams told me: *"Didn't I tell you? Run with them and become them."* I was just like Ashley and Kevin and the rest of them boys on Guilford. I kept thinking how dumb I must really be, to end up in a lineup. Turn this way, and now that. It was like we were behind a two-way mirror, or some faux wall. We were being judged. I could feel it.

A cop came from behind a door. I imagined they had some white women back there picking us out. When an officer approached us, he said, "This one." My heart was pounding.

I mumbled a confused, "Me?"

I knew what this meant for my life. I knew I'd be branded. I seen it before. Once they get you in the system, they never stop trying to pin some crime on you. My heart raced when he reached out to grab me. I was done. I lifted my head in acceptance. It was my fault, because I knew better. I shouldn't'na been out here like that. I shoulda listened to Mama. My heart was beating faster than it ever had but I had to accept it.

Just when I thought the officer was gonna grab me, he grabbed Ashley's arm. Ashley smiled. I swear there was something wrong with him. I didn't understand him. I wanted to know what was so damn funny.

The officer said, "Purse snatcher."

Ashley laughed. It was like he was in a world of his own. This was serious, but he just kept smiling.

The officer angered. "You think this is a joke?"

"I ain't snatch no bitch purse, but I wish I did."

Ashley just kept smiling and walking like he was accepting some kind of award.

The officer yanked Ashley toward a room at the back of the police station. "Come on," he demanded.

In my mind, I kept seeing prison cells like those on television, thinking about how they were gonna lock him up back there.

As he was leading Ashley away, Ashley said, "Yall think I'm scared. I ain't scared."

I let out a breath so loud everyone looked at me. I was scared for him.

***

They kept us in that police station all night. Mama was supposed to work a double but when they called, she came to the police station looking like she wanted to kill me. I couldn't even look at her. Mama was mean, her eyes were nasty. I could tell she wanted to choke the life out of me. I ain't even make eye contact with her.

She said, "Can't believe I gotta miss work for this shit. Yo black ass know better. You know I got a lotta bills to pay. Gotta feed yo stupid ass. You think they gon' pay me for coming to get yo stupid ass? I shoulda told them to keep yo dumb ass in here."

Naomi came in behind Mama. "Where's Ashley?" she asked.

"They took him in the back."

Kevin was bent over looking hungry. "Dude choked him out."

Naomi was horrified. "Choked him out? Who?" Naomi kept trying to talk to the police about Ashley being choked out, but they denied it.

"He snatched a purse, ma'am."

She was real upset. They kept asking who she was.

"I'm his sister." She was irate. She was yelling. "I wanna know who put their hands on him. He's a child. He's only fifteen. I wanna see him. Where is he? Bring him to me, now."

They said she couldn't see him because his gran'ma was his real guardian and she had to come if Ashley was to be released.

Mama was mad as hell. She kept telling me I knew better. She slapped me. "God knows I want to kill yo black ass."

The cops was laughing at me. "Don't kill him."

They charged Ashley with that purse snatching. They charged him as an adult. They said the girl hurt her arm real bad, and it's his fault. They said she had to have surgery on her tendons.

Mama didn't even look at me like I was JuJu no more. I was fortunate, though. No one came to pick up Kevin, so they put him in a group home.

When I was in the backseat Mama just kept looking at me. Naomi was in the front seat, crying. "Why won't they let me see him. They probably beatin' him right now."

I wanted to talk to her. I wanted to tell her he was gon' be alright, but Mama kept watching me in the rearview. I could see it in her eyes, that Mama hated me. It was like I was gon' be her biggest failure.

While we was headed home, Mama said, "I just don't know what to say. I don't even know you." I felt bad. I let her down. I let myself down.

"What'd I do to you? Why you hate me so much? You used to be a good son."

"I don't hate you."

"You can't keep blaming me. Is that why you do all this?"

"No."

"I know you think it's my fault he left."

"No, I don't."

"Listen, I love you JuJu. But I don't know what's wrong with you. You don't care."

"Yes, I do."

"No, you don't, cuz if you did, you'd see how hard it is. You'd see how hard I work. I don't want this for you. I don't want my son to be no janitor. Or in jail. God made you smart for a reason. You not like yo friends, or yo brothers. I could see if you was dumb. I could see if you didn't know no better, but you do. You know more than anybody I ever met. You's the smartest man I ever talked to in my whole life. Even my boss ain't smart like you."

"I'm not smart. The kids at school tell me I'm dumb. Even my teachers think I'm dumb."

"Stop it. Don't do that. Don't. They told me you keep pretending you can't read so they won't ask you nothin'. I know you can read. I see you reading that *Mockingbird* book. I know you've read it a hundred times by now. I don't know why you pretend like you dumb. If I was smart like you, I'd want everybody to know it. You just keep changin'. You just so different now. You lying all the time. Stealing. Running 'round with them hoodlums. What happened to you, I don't know. I thought you was gon' be somethin'."

I didn't know what to say.

Mama backed into the driveway. "You gon' have to fix this on your own. I can't keep chasing you like this. I don't know what to do anymore. I mean, you're a teenager. I'm just tired of takin' yo shit, JuJu. I am. I really am. You want to throw it all away? I won't stop you no more." She got out and went in the house.

I sat there for a minute. When I got out, I saw my sisters in the window. It just hit me. It was the look in their eye. Especially Boo. It was like they stopped seeing me, the real me. It was like I was just another dumb nigger from the ghetto, and it bothered me. It hurt me. It ate my insides. It wasn't what I wanted. I was just having fun.

When I got inside Morris was standing in the kitchen. "What they charge you with?"

"Nothin'. I don't know."

Sean came downstairs shaking his head. "What'd I tell you, boy? You ain't no criminal. Keep yo little ass in school."

Morris said, "I tried to tell him."

28

They eventually let Ashley out of the police station at like 3:00 in the morning. His gran'ma had to go and sign for him. It took a lot out of her. She ain't never come home after Ashley got arrested. They said she was in one of them homes for old people.

The morning after we got arrested, my father pulled up out front. My father was a tall, thin, light-skinned black man who his Deep South friends called Red and his friends in the north called JJ. It's always like that in the ghetto. People never call you by your real name.

People was scared of my father like they scared of Morris. He wasn't no fighter. He carried a pistol. Rumors told my father used his pistol many times in pool halls and on street corners. He was a Korean War vet. Mama told us one time he woke up screaming telling her about how his unit killed a village of women and children. He was also a heroin addict—and Mama said it was because of them women and children he killed in Korea. Said his superiors shot him up because he would scream all night about them women and children they killed.

He was a gambler. He sold pills and codeine cough syrup. He had a long, deep, reliable reputation. He was respected, but really everybody was scared of him. Even Mama. When they was still together, he knocked Mama teeth out. They was in the kitchen and Mama was cooking dinner. My father had a sweet tooth and Mama ain't have nothing to drink, except water. Mama gave him a glass of water and he left the table with a frown. I could see Mama looking like she did something wrong. Looking like she was his slave or somethin'. My father put his glass in her face.

"You ain't got no Kool-Aid or nothin'?"

Mama shook her head, like a child.

"Put some sugar in it or somethin', shit."

"You don't need all that sugar."

"Fuck you gon' tell me what I need?"

"Look, you ain't got to cuss me in front of my kids."

"Since you working you just smart now, ain't'cha?"

"I make my own money."

"Just talkin' back. Who you fuckin'?"

"What? Ain't you got more sense than that? You know'd I ain't been with nobody but my husban' before I met you."

"You gon' quit talkin' back to me like that. Now get me some motha fuckin' sugar."

"Get yo own sugar. Talk all that in front of my kids."

"What? What you say to me?" He grabbed Mama by the arm.

"Let go of me."

Mama pulled away. My father broke his glass of water on the floor. He smacked my mama with the back of his hand. Mama dug her nails into his face.

"Bitch."

My father punched Mama right in her mouth like she was a man. Mama screamed and fell to the floor, her mouth bloody. My sisters started crying. My heart jumped. My father looked at the dining table. Morris, Sean, and Terrence stood. Mama was shaking her head for them not to get involved. They ain't do nothing. My father already pulled a gun on they father, so they was scared of him too.

Mama spit her teeth out right on the floor. My father squatted next to her. "Oh baby." Mama pushed him away. My father lifted his hand like he wanted to caress Mama's face. Mama flinched. She was scared. She just knew his fist was coming. He said, "Baby, I ain't gon' hurt you." He touched her face. Mama was all scared of his hand like it was a trick.

I went and got her a rag. My heart was beating real bad. My father tried to touch my shoulder, but I knocked his hand off.

He got his plate and left for his car.

Mama didn't know what to do. She wanted to call the police, but she didn't. My aunt brought her a shotgun. She couldn't even go to sleep unless that shotgun was near her.

My father would come from time to time to get a look at me, his youngest son. I was his only son who hadn't been arrested. He would tell me all about how it was Mama's fault. Mama would never blame him because she had cheated on her husband when she conceived me, so she blamed herself, though my father was married to another woman too. Mama begged God to forgive her.

After a while she started dating. My father would come by and scare them off if Mama was getting too close to them. When he darkened the door them other men would just squeeze out, they head down, begging my father's pardon. They'd make up for a couple days. Then he met a younger woman and left Mama for good.

This morning, I had to go sit in his passenger seat and talk to him. He's always in different cars; this morning he was driving a red BMW.

"You snatchin' purses?"

"I ain't snatch no purse."

"You think that ain't gon' get back to me?"

"I ain't snatch no purse."

"You stealin'?" He looked at me. He could tell I was. "If they ever get me for stealing, I better be stealing Fort Knox. Do no time for no petty beef. What's wrong wit you? If they gon' put you in jail make 'em put you in there for stealin' something that gon' set yo Mama up fo life."

"Just got caught up."

"What they charge you with?"

"I don't know. Nothin'."

After my father left Mama made me walk to the Super Duper on Broadway to get her some flour. When I got up there it was like 8:30 in the morning. Elijah's Cadillac was parked in the lot. I saw him take a swig from a beer can. I knew it was him because he always wore that WWII Vet cap. He said wearing that cap was the only way to keep police from pulling him over.

I always liked Elijah. He was cool. He showed me how to use a blow torch when the hot water tank died. He showed me how to change out the electrical switches when we lived on Humboldt Parkway. He even taught me how to barbeque real good while Mama was at work. He was gon' teach me how to drive before they broke up.

When I got to his window, he just shook his head like he was disappointed in me. He pointed to his skull. He rolled the window down. "What happened?"

"I don't know. I was stupid."

"What they charge you with?"

"I don't know. Why everybody keep asking me that?"

"Cuz they cuff you for one thing and because they can't prove it, or because you innocent, they charge you with resisting. Every black man gets charged with resisting now. Yo turn comin', if they ain't already done it. That's how they get you in the system. That's how they get yo fingerprints."

Elijah used to say it don't matter what a black man thinks he is, "because society has already given us black man syndrome." That's what he called it. He explained it to me one time that all black men—but especially those tall like me—are in danger, because there is an expectation set upon us down from slavery and Jim Crow, which says we are violent and tough and strong. No matter our personality or career or societal positioning, we are a threat. A physical threat. A physical threat which must be dealt with physically. Elijah would say, "Normal male aggression is seen as violent behavior in black men, but not in white men." He was telling me how white people create loopholes in the law for aggressive white boys. He said, "Whites just stopped arresting white boys for rape. They charge them with 'date rape' instead of rape." Elijah kept telling me I was too smart to get arrested. He was really disappointed in me. I could feel it. I could see it in his eyes. All I could do is look at the ground.

When I came back with Mama's flour, Corey came out her bedroom and said, "What they charge you with, resisting?"

Mama ain't say nothin'. She refused to talk to me. In fact, I ain't talk to Mama again until my court date.

We went together, me, Ashley, Mama, and Naomi. At court, we saw Kevin with the white people responsible for him now. They was like priests or something. He nodded but we couldn't speak. They had us in this big hallway with half the boys in the neighborhood. One boy after another went in and got yelled at. When it was my turn, I knew what to expect. The guy was some administrator. He just sat there all old and white and balding, yelling at me for about ten minutes, telling me I knew better and whatever.

He asked me, "What'd you want to be?"

"A writer. I want to write a book."

He just looked at me. He was confused. *I'm supposed to be a bad black. I'm supposed to think about crime.*

"Yeah, what was the last book you finished?"

"*To Kill a Mockingbird.*"

He smiled like I was lying. "How did it end?"

"After that racist broke Jem's arm, Boo Radley saved him."

He gave me a nod. "Well, let this be a lesson to you. You ain't gon' be no writer from behind bars. These kids you hang 'round, they ain't got bright futures."

People keep saying that. That we ain't got no chance. That there ain't no hope for our future. I don't like it. I don't want to agree with it. Even if inside I knew it was true.

I couldn't look at him no more. Not because I was mad. Because I didn't want to believe it. *We gon' make it out of here. We gon' look back at being young and stupid and laugh while we at the cookout.*

He started screaming at me again.

Ashley had to have a real court date for snatching that purse he didn't snatch. We ain't snatch that purse, we really didn't. We wasn't that stupid to get caught. Ashley showed us his technique, which was to walk behind a white woman and wait for the right time to cut the purse strap and be halfway home before she knew we'd cut the strap. We ain't even snatch no purses though because we got arrested before we could.

When we went to his real court date, Naomi made him wear a suit she got from Goodwill. He was mad about it. Naomi said, "You can't go looking like no thief."

His court date was over fast because his lawyer told him if he pleads guilty, he wouldn't have to go to juvy. They also said no one would look into Naomi being his caregiver if he pleaded guilty. Ashley kept saying, "I ain't do it," but they convinced Naomi. He kept saying, "Tell 'em, JuJu. Tell 'em it wasn't us." They ain't care what we said. They had Ashley pegged for it. They told Naomi he wouldn't have a record if he pleads guilty, because they'd seal it.

His alcoholic looking public defender said, "If he don't get in trouble again before he turn sixteen. It would be like it never happened." Ashley pled guilty. The whole thing was just bad.

I ain't hang out with Ashley and the rest of them for almost two weeks. When I did get back out there on the stoop, Ashley was different. He ain't care about nothin' no more. He said, "It don't matter, because I'm guilty anyway. No matter what, to white people we already guilty." He said, "White people already made up their mind."

29

After we got arrested, I spent most of my time in the house. One day when I returned to my bedroom after playing spades with my sisters Sean was standing inside my bedroom reading a magazine I got from school.

"Where you get this?"

"School."

"They gave this to y'all in school?"

"Yeah, why?"

"Let me hold it. I'a give it back."

I nodded.

That Scholastic magazine is the last thing I got at the end of the school year. It was in a class with a teacher, Andrea, who don't like me. She the one who told Mama I called her a bitch. Well, Andrea *is* a bitch. She got mad because she misspelled *alcohol* on the chalkboard for our spelling test and I corrected her. One time in social studies she told us, "The reason the world is better without Hitler is because, if Hitler had the bomb, he woulda used it." I raised my hand. She frowned. She didn't like when I asked questions.

Before she could deny me, I said, "*We* used the bomb. What does that say about *us*?"

"That was different. We were defending ourselves."

"We used the bomb because we were losing—"

When I said that, she told me, "Oh, shut up."

My classmates were laughing at me, especially the white kids. She had this amused look on her face. She frowned and rocked her head like she got the best of me. That's what she always did to me. Whenever I asked a question, she'd make me feel so small, I'd stop asking questions. My teachers ain't really like me. I was just a little nigger boy they had to deal with between paychecks. At least that's how I felt.

The Montessori school I went to is full of mumbo jumbo. Honestly the only thing worth learning from a Montessori school is reason and perspective, both of which I have become completely trained in. I have become so fascinated by perspective that I have trained myself in the ability of putting my soul in the body of another and understanding life from his perspective. It is something that works well, unless you live in the ghetto. If you live in the ghetto, this gift is seen as a curse, where you are accused of "being soft," or "thinking too much." Thinking too much, pausing, understanding the other guy's perspective makes you a punk.

Anyway, my teachers ain't never really like me but it ain't start going real bad until I started getting into fights. One time when I was staring this kid down, making sure he didn't swing on me, Andrea got mad because I didn't respond to her yelling. When this stupid fool sat down, I turned to Andrea.

"Fuck you," she said, and walked away.

I didn't care. I already knew she didn't like me. Another time this kid kept waving his dollar in my face, so I snatched it.

"Give it back. It's for my lunch."

I ain't give him nothin'. He went running to get Andrea. She came out looking mean, but I didn't care. I seen a lot of mean faces. Mean faces from teachers don't mean nothin' to me no more. I hid his dollar in my sock.

Andrea ain't find nothin'. She had to give the kid a dollar or he wouldn't be able to eat lunch.

These teachers are all con artists to me now. They just pretending to care about us, but they don't care if we learn, I can tell. They just want to get through their daily script and go home. I started getting into trouble all the time and Andrea had it out for me. She would just come and grab my arm and tell me I was in trouble. School wasn't fun for me at all.

One day Andrea started yelling at me and a group of guys, telling us our voices were too deep. She said we were becoming men. She said we should shut our mouths, because she could hear us "whispering." She said, "Especially you, JuJu."

I don't even have a deep voice. "It wasn't me."

"Yes, it was. I know your voice."

"No, it wasn't. I'll tell you everything that was said."

This kid named Russell pushed me in the shoulder. He didn't want me to tell. We were talking about a movie on the Playboy channel. In the movie, Cinderella's fairy godfather gave her a special power, so the prince wouldn't forget her. We was talking about it, laughing over it. Russell was one of the toughest kids in the Montessori school. Whenever he got in trouble Andrea came and found me because she kept saying I was "the ringleader." Because I knew better. It was bullshit, if you want to know the truth. I hated it. Andrea was always blaming me no matter what.

One time, Russell had this girl trying to have sex with him in school. They kept using me as "the negotiator." I was helping, I'm not gonna lie. It was my idea they skip out on swim class and sneak into the boys' bathroom, down in the basement. He was scared, so I came as a lookout. While we was waiting for the girl, he took a condom out of his pocket and said, "She bet not be playin'. If she come down here, I'ma put this on and make her give me some pussy."

"Dude you can't take it, she gotta give it to you. Plus, she like you anyway. You can't rape her, man."

He started laughin'.

Another one of our classmates heard us talkin' so he came in wearing his swim trunks asking who Russell was gonna rape.

"Nobody while I'm here."

This third dude, Kareem, was from one of them Nation of Islam families. I was lucky he came because after the girl showed us her breasts, we got caught by the janitor. Kareem refused to blame me. He told them I said no one can rape the girl. They took it easy on me because of Kareem. I only got three days' suspension. The other three, including the girl, got seven days. They even made them see a psychiatrist. They told Mama I said Russell can't rape the girl. I protect my sisters and that's why I wouldn't let him rape her.

A lot of the women teachers would smile at me or pat my back for this, but Andrea didn't care. She was meaner than she was before. She kept saying it was my fault and I understood what I was doing. She tried to say those other kids went along because they wanted me to like them. She was adamant I be kicked out of the Montessori school. Well, I wasn't kicked out because they said I prevented a rape.

While I was on suspension Mama made Joe Bolden, my brothers' father and her out-of-work ex-husband, stay with me so I didn't get into trouble. I told him it was fine if he took the ten dollars Mama paid him and left, but he didn't. He pointed his mean old finger and said, "Go sit down." He came back to Mama for a year, after my father left. He was always grabbing me with his sandpaper hands telling me, "Do as you're told," especially if I wasn't paying attention. I would hear him asking Mama if he could whoop my ass. He was a tough-ass. He served in Vietnam and worked twenty years at Republic Steel, before it shut down. Now he just smokes cigarettes, coughs, and does odd jobs where he can.

When I was suspended, he just sat there smoking and watching TV, with his beady little eyes. One time we was talking about what happened with Kelly, that girl we had showing us her breasts in the boy's bathroom. I told him it wasn't my fault.

He said, "Don't matter if it's yo fault. You was there." He said, "Yo Mama told me you was smart. You had a uncle on yo mama side who was a real smart man. He used to write programs for the church. He got a printing business out of it. Well if you is smart, you should know it don't matter if it was yo fault or not. If I rob a bank and you waiting outside, ain't you going to jail too?"

"Nah. I'ma tell 'em I ain't have nothing to do with it. I'ma say you told me you was making a deposit."

He just laughed. "You gon' learn."

The news came on and he wanted to watch Irv Weinstein. There was a story of a sixteen-year-old in trouble for purse snatching. Some kid snatched a purse and they gave him the maximum sentence. They also gave the maximum to his friend. Joe Bolden shook his head.

"See. Don't matter if you did anything. You was there. They make a law of being there because they know poor boys run in packs. They gon' get you in prison. That's they new thang. Lock up all the young in prison. Get the system on you. You gon' see when they get you behind them bars. You think you just gon' explain something away but you ain't. You ain't no kid to them. That's what you don't understand. In their eyes, you already a man.

To them, even at twelve or thirteen, you's a man. They gon' treat you like a man. Put you behind bars like a man. Even yo mama gon' call you 'the man of the house,' because black people been trained to understand black children grown as soon as they start walkin'. They gon' call you grown and mannish and all that shit, even when you just a baby. See, back in slavery they made black children adults at five, so they could work 'em in the fields. Ain't no such thing as a black child to them. That's still they view of black children, today. Well you ain't no man. You's a child. I don't care what y'all don with that girl in the bathroom. That don't make you a man. You understand what I'm telling you?"

"Yeah."

"Do you?"

I thought I did.

He started the "you have'ta's," and I hate all of them "You have'ta's," that came from black people. It's always a rule of law—or a rule of white people—that I must obey or be locked up, or kicked out, or barred. *"You have'ta do this or white people will judge you."* That's all I ever heard. *"Be this way for white people to like you."* It's always what I must do so white people don't think poorly of me, even if they ain't know me. I couldn't never just be me. I couldn't never just be free. I couldn't never just be making mistakes. They always act like I'm planning a con on them. They always act like I'm some all-knowing black charlatan. But that's how it is. They think black boys know the same thing as black men. They treat you like you're trying to trick them and that you have every answer in the book. I had to always think about how white people was viewing me. They was always telling me how to act around white people and what to do if white people have the wrong impression of me. It was a lot of pressure. You have to always be a step ahead of them, so they didn't make assumptions about how bad you is. They keep telling you, you have to smile and be happy and keep white people at ease. You have to always be pleading yo case about how you is a "good black." I was sick of it. I ain't want to make myself in a fake image for white people. I ain't want people to always think I was thinking about crime, but that's what white people do. They go around and treat us like we up to no good, even if we ain't. Especially cops. They called the cops on Mama because we drove through a good neighborhood.

Mama drove us through a rich neighborhood because she was mad I got suspended. She said I was "going down the wrong path."

My sisters kept saying, "That's my house. That's my house. I'ma have a house just like that, Mama."

At first, I didn't care and then I said, "I'ma buy you that house right there, Mama."

I said I was gon' be rich. Mama just laughed.

She said, "Bet you forget about yo poor ole mama when you get rich."

"No, I ain't. I'ma buy you a big house right next to all the white people so they can get mad."

It was the biggest house on the street, I promised to buy Mama. She asked how I was gon' do that and I said, "I'ma be rich." Mama was laughing real good.

While we was out there dreaming about big houses, the police pulled us over. The cop said they got a call Mama that was "casing houses."

"Doing what?" Mama was mad when them cops explained it to her. "You gotta be jokin'."

They kept looking at me in the front seat.

"That's my son. He ain't nothin' but thirteen."

They looked at me again like Mama was lying.

I was scared. I ain't look at 'em one time. I kept my eyes on the floor like Mama always told me I had to. I ain't make no moves. I kept my hands on my knees. That ain't stop me from being mad, resentful and bitter about the way they watched me, 'bout the way they judged me. I knew they was my enemy, I could feel it in my soul. It's the way they look at you when you a black boy. It's like y'all in a war against each other. It's like they want to drag you off and lock you in the stockade, just for being black. It's like everything you is is wrong, bad, evil and black, when they looking at you like that.

I could tell Mama was scared, too. Mama started giving the police her black resume. That's what old black people call it when blacks try to prove they ain't no criminal and start naming all they accomplishments because they don't want to be seen as no bad black. They be thinking officers won't beat you or arrest you if you ain't no bad black.

Mama said she was working since she was five. "I have a son in the military. We poor, Officer, but we ain't criminals." She said, "Look Officer, you think I'a be out here committing crimes with my kids in the car? It's my day off." Mama gave him her work ID. "I took my kids to get some ice cream and over here to look at houses. We'll leave."

He got Mama's license. He looked at all of her stickers in the windshield. After he was convinced Mama ain't a bad black, he let us go.

Mama was real mad. She was driving and wiping a tear from her eye. "They don't care. This ain't what Dr. King died for, so they can judge us. We supposed to be free now. I dun pick all they cotton and washed all they clothes and raised up all they babies and they still act like I'm some black monster. I ain't doing nothing but driving. I can't even drive or they callin' the law. You can't be here. You can't be there. God, I'm sick of it."

When we got to the light Mama looked at me. She rubbed her hand down my forehead. She shook my shoulder and let out a bunch of air. She looked at my sisters.

"Y'all alright?"

"Yeah."

***

When school was almost over Andrea was all high and mighty telling me how dumb I was. She stuffed a paper I wrote in my face because I got a failing grade. "Remember this?"

I did remember. *I'll always remember. So, I got it wrong. It says more about you than me. I'm a kid. If I didn't learn from you, what does that say about you? You're the teacher. Not me.* I was thinking all of that. I wanted to say it. I didn't. I was biting my teeth. I was thinking about snatching that paper.

She pushed it into my chest. She wiped her tears. She said, "I'll see you for eighth grade, next year."

I hate teachers like Andrea. They always act like you're not even alive. Like you're not a thinking human being. They always treat you like you're black. *I know I'm from the ghetto. I know you don't have any hope for my life. I know you think I'll never be as good as you. But I'm still fighting for a better life. I still want to be somebody. I'm gonna be a writer.*

I had this teacher named Alison who was real nice. She always seemed to care about what you was feeling and let you talk to her like you were both people. She ain't never talk down to you or make you feel stupid. It was like she believed if you didn't understand, it was her fault. She walked up to me while I was steaming on the bench and said, "What are you doing?"

"Sittin' on the bench."

"No, I mean, what are you doing?"

She meant with my life. I didn't know how to answer.

"Think about it. You're smarter than this."

I did think about it. I'll probably never stop thinking about it. Or her.

At the end of June, Andrea handed out that Scholastic magazine Sean wanted to borrow. First, they had them DARE cops come talk to us about drugs. Andrea read an article in the magazine on how to make a new drug called crack. It told all the ingredients needed to make crack: baking soda, cocaine, and water. All of us thought it was funny to name a drug crack. One kid said, "This my new drug, butt crack, you want some?" The class laughed.

Andrea finished reading and talking about crack as an "epidemic." When she finished, she told us the magazine was ours to keep.

30

You always think that you gon' make it out. I told myself I wasn't even no bad kid. I told myself it wasn't my fault. I thought it was the police who were the real problem. "I didn't even do nothin'." That was my favorite line whenever I was asked what happened.

I needed to take reasonability like Mama said, but I didn't. I couldn't. The ghetto was changing so fast. What we did seems like boyhood innocence. Just good rebelling against the system. Against parents. Against American morals. It was just kid stuff. Poor kid stuff. We was just surviving. *We was just kids born into a rotten system.* Anyway, that's how I wrote it in my notebook.

Yesterday morning when I was headed to the bathroom to pee, I opened the door without knocking. I saw Corey smoking crack.

I don't even know how it happened, but one day crack just exploded in the ghetto. Everybody was saying Ronald Reagan was trying to stop the upward momentum of black people in the country same as he did as governor of California. They was saying Reagan was trying to starve us out. That he wanted to make the black man worse off than the poorest white man. They said he had the military and CIA dumping guns and crack into the ghetto. Don't nobody know how it happened. One day it just started showing up. Tons of it. It wasn't organic. We wasn't cooking it at first. It was just showing up ready to smoke.

Corey was mad I saw him smoking. "Don't be opening no doors without knocking, motha fucka. Fuck wrong with you, bitch. I mighta had my dick in my hand. I should kick yo skinny ass. What is you retarded or something?" He was real mad. He ain't want nobody to know he was smoking crack. Especially Mama.

When they first started smoking crack, them addicts didn't want nobody to know about it. They was sneaking around smoking that shit, trying to keep normal. That crack ain't help them keep it secret though because they got skinny. Real skinny, like they was starving to death. The crack dealers was the same in the beginning. They ain't want to be drug dealers. Some of them was still working their day job, but after a couple of weeks the ghetto was on fire with dealers and smokers doing crazy shit for crack money. The ghetto ain't the same no more. The ghetto is a place for crime and that crack everybody selling now. Every black boy I knew was a crack dealer now. Even Morris and Sean sell crack over on Herman Street. Morris didn't even work his job no more.

When Mama asked him why he quit he said, "Cuz I like what I'm doing."

Mama said, "And what's that, being a criminal?"

"Gettin' money."

After he said that he gave Mama $1,000.

I thought Mama wasn't gon' take it cuz her face was wrinkled bad. He was just holding it in his hand. Mama was just looking at Morris and Sean, standing there with their new clothes and sneakers and sunglasses, like they was movie stars.

Sean said, "Take it Mama. You know you need it."

She did too because every year when she bought us notebooks and school clothes, they turned off our lights. Every September. Sometimes it even happened in July, if Mama drove us to Alabama to see our great aunt Frances, our oldest living relative.

Corey was watching from the couch. He said, "Take it babe, shid, I don't turn down nothin' but my collar."

Mama took it. She hurried it in her pocket like she was gon' get in trouble. It was all the encouragement Sean and Morris needed. It was all the encouragement I needed. You don't think you like them but seeing how people treat them gets to you. You think I want to be the son taking care of things. You think I want to get the new clothes and sunglasses so people think I'm somebody. You think even white people will treat you like a somebody if you dressed like that. If you look expensive. You think I can go out the ghetto and police will see I'm somebody and leave me alone. It don't never work like that.

This morning when I came out my bedroom, Sean was putting a padlock on the bedroom door across from me.

"What you doing that for? You movin' back in?"

"Don't let nobody in here. You hear me? Not even Mama." He added, "Oh yeah. When I was coming in the door, old dude told me to give you this." It was two bus tokens. "Said you supposed to visit his son."

When I got out there, I tried to get in to see Kevin, but one of the priests stopped me.

"Can I help you?"

"My friend stay here. Kevin. Kevin Barber."

"Kevin. He's here, but he can't have visitors."

I let out a breath.

"But," he continued, "I'll let him come out and talk to you for ten minutes. This is against the rules. I'll make this one exception. You're the only person to visit him since he's been here. Even his mother don't visit. I told her I'd pick her up and she hung up on me. His father won't even answer when I call. I stopped trying to get them to come, thinking they'd come on their own, when they can. So far, they haven't. Wait here."

I sat on their giant concrete step, waiting, just watching traffic. I was counting cars. I was watching for which car I would drive when I get out of Buffalo and become a writer. Drivers looked at me like I ain't belong in north Buffalo. North Buffalo is middle-class and upper-middle class. It's also where Buffalo has some of its biggest homes. There's a lot of good neighborhoods, mostly Italian and Jewish.

While I was zoned out watching cars, I heard Kevin say, "Yo, my man? Yo Ash…" When he saw it was me, he said, "What up JuJu?" He was looking around, but it was just me. Just me and him. None of our friends came. No one visited him. Like that priest said, not even his mother.

He had on some tight clothes and some white buddies. He gained some weight like he was eating good. I was smiling at his haircut. He always gave himself bad haircuts, but this haircut was funny. Kevin had one of them fake haircuts, like an inmate cut it. He had one of them lines cut in the side, but that joint was too wide.

"What's up man?" I said with a grin.

"What?" he replied.

"Nothin' man. Just lookin' at you."

"What, I look different?"

"Shid. They got you lookin' like you just did a bid."

"Man, g'on 'head with that."

I couldn't stop laughin'. He laughed with me.

"How they treatin' you?"

"Who, these dudes? Man, they cool and shit. They feed a brotha good, know what I'm saying?" He showed off his belly. We laughed. He had a real serious grimace. "Where Ashley?"

"He chillin', man."

"Word? He can't come see me?"

"I tried."

"Knew this dude since I was six. Bump him if it's like that."

"It ain't like that."

"Bump that." His brow was wrinkled real bad.

"What's good with'chu? What they got'chu doing out here?"

"Shid, nothin'. Keep a brotha locked up. Curfew and all that shit like that. They got me out here trying to get on a team."

"Football?"

"Yeah. I'a probably wait ta next year doe. They make it hard out here. Paperwork, and all kind of rules I gotta follow. Be here. Be there. Can't be here. Can't be there." He let out a breath.

"Seen yo pops."

"Man, bump him."

"Told him I was trying to get out here. Gave me a couple tokens."

"Word. He probably got them joints from the welfare."

"Sayin', I think he still care. Know what I'm sayin'?"

"Bump him. I can't stay with him anyway. I told them about that time when he punched me in my face. They said it ain't a good idea for me to stay there. Told 'em how I pulled a knife on him one time. Plus, they said he'd have to get a two bedroom. Pops ain't trying to do nothin' but get drunk. Ever since Moms divorced him, he ain't been doing nothin' but getting drunk. That's it, getting drunk and chasing stragglers."

"Right. Right."

"Shid the other day, they had this dude who used to stay here come talk to us—a Marine. Said Buffalo fucked up and you ain't gon' know Buffalo fucked up, until you leave Buffalo. Been thinking about joining."

***

When I got home Boo told me, "Sean looking for you."

"What he want?"

"I don't know. Go see."

When I got over there, a line of crack addicts was coming out the back door of Morris' apartment, like they was waiting on Jesus or somethin'.

When I went inside Morris and Sean were in the kitchen cooking crack. Sean was reading that Scholastic magazine I got from the Montessori school, with that crack recipe in it. Morris was selling crack out the back door. They had to squeeze me in because smokers was trying to get in. Morris had to rack his shotgun, so they'd stop pulling my shirt.

Morris said, "Where you been?"

"Went to see Kevin."

"If we need you here, be yo ass here. I need you to do something for me." He looked at Sean. "Give him the bag."

They had a gym bag. It was kinda heavy, like if my school bag had two books in it.

"Take this and put it in my room," Morris said.

"They gon' see me."

Morris went and looked out the front window. He came back. They taped their drug money around my waist, front and back. Sean gave me the key.

Morris said, "Go straight home."

Sean said, "Don't stop for nobody."

Morris grabbed my arm as I started toward the door. "Don't stop for nobody. Don't talk to nobody. Hit the shortcut."

When I was coming out the shortcut, I saw Ashley sell crack to a smoker.

When I went in Mama said, "What's that smell?" I thought she was gon' say I smelled like outside, but she didn't. "What is that?" I hurried and put their drug money under their mattress. When I was leaving, Mama said, "That smell again. What is it?" I figured it was me. I figured I smelled like that crack Morris and Sean was cooking. I smelled my shirt. I couldn't smell nothin'.

***

At night when I was sleeping, it just started. I woke startled. When I went downstairs Mama was sitting in darkness looking out the window. My sisters woke up. We was just in the living room listening to it.

Mama said, "You think they den started a race war?"

Black people in Mama generation, those who lived through colored drinking fountains, was always worried white people would decide it was time to bring back segregation, and was always worried white people would use a race war.

Corey said, "Hell naw, they ain't start no race war."

Mama didn't believe him. Mama kept watching the curtains like white Southerners was gon' come and snatch her back to sharecropping. I ain't never see that kind of fear on Mama like I seen when she was scared white people had decided to return her to the South, to pick cotton.

All through the night, it kept going. Gunshot after gunshot. Siren after siren. Mama became worried about Sean and Morris. "I wish they was home." She told me to call them. They ain't answer.

In the morning when the news came on, three black boys had been killed, another five had been shot.

The ghetto ain't safe no more. People crazy now. It's this crack, and this crack money. You have to watch yo back now. You have to watch black boys like they a war enemy. Sometimes when I'm walking down the street, I feel them watching me. They think I'm making crack money. They think I got a gun. They think I want to rob them of their crack money. They think I want their crack spot. I fear them more than I fear the police, now. I fear them like Mama fear them white Southerners.

One time this dude just walked up beside me and put his pistol in my hip. He grabbed my shirt so tight I felt his knuckles in my chest.

"You hustlin'?"

"No."

He checked my pockets. Morris told me not to never keep no money in my pockets no more. When he seen I ain't have nothing he took his gun off my hip. I took off running.

I ran to Morris' apartment. There was a line longer than for free lunch. Them smokers was all looking at me like I could help them. I didn't like it. They kept saying, "Give me a hit. Give me a hit baby." I didn't like it. I didn't like when they looked at me. I didn't like when they knew me. They was grabbing me. They said, "Give me a hit. Please." They kept touching me. I didn't want them to know me.

"Don't touch me. Fuck off me."

One said, "C'mon, JuJu?"

"How the fuck you know my name?"

He was just smiling. These people knew me. They watched me grow up. These were my people, and I was helping in their demise. I pulled away from them. Sean squeezed me in the door.

I was telling him, "Dude pulled a gun on me."

Morris said, "Who?" He pulled out an AK47. I didn't want them to catch a murder charge.

"I don't know. Some dude. He took off running."

"You don't know him? His face, or nothin'?"

"Nah."

I did know his face. I seen him before but I acted like I didn't.

Morris dropped me off at the house, driving a white Toyota Land Cruiser he bought last week. When we parked in front of the house he said, "You sure you ain't recognize dude?"

"I don't know him. I didn't see his face."

Morris was looking around watching everyone. He was watching every car and everyone walking down the street. I was watching Ashley sell crack off his stoop.

"Take this and put it in my room." He gave me the key. "And bring the key back when you finish."

I took his gym bag inside and put it under one of them twin beds. When Morris left, I went and sat on the stoop with Ashley. We sold crack all night.

When I went home Corey was sitting on the couch. He watched until I was out of sight. When I was almost upstairs, Mama was trying to figure out what the smell was.

"You smell that?"

Corey said, "I don't smell nothin'."

I went in my room. I woke up because I couldn't sleep with all the chatter outside my window. When I looked, there was fifty or sixty men and women outside Ashley's door asking for crack. They was demanding crack. I thought they was gon' break in Ashley's house and take what they wanted.

I watched from my bedroom window. I just kept looking at them. I felt like that black dude in *Dawn of the Dead*. It was like most of them wasn't even alive no more. I saw some of my friends' mothers, and their fathers and brothers, and sisters, and cousins. I saw so many people I recognized.

I finally got back to sleep.

31

Sometimes the ghetto just comes for you. Even if you not truly involved. Once you "take up with the wrong crowd," as Mama calls it, it's too late to back out. You can't never say, "I'm just hanging around, I'm not like him." It's like Mr. Williams and Mama ex-husband was telling me: If you *with* them, to people on the outside, you *are* them. Ain't no room to say "This my best friend, he hustlin'. I'm not."

This morning, me and Ashley was selling crack off his stoop. These dudes started standing around at the corner. I saw them. I had a bad feeling.

I was like, "Who that?"

Ashley said, "Smokers."

"Nah man." I stood. I saw one of them had a pipe and another had a club. Ashley had that bat in his doorway.

When he turned to pick it up, they was on us, fast. They robbed us. They was older than us. They musta been in their twenties. Shit, they mighta been in they thirties.

They was serious. They was hitting us with their fists and with pipes all in our shoulders and stomachs and thighs. We held out. One of them punched me so hard he opened a cut under my right eye.

"Where the shit at?" he demanded.

Blood splashed onto my eyeball, so it shut immediately. I musta been in shock 'cause I thought I was crying and hollering, but I wasn't. The blood was coming out too fast. It was like dripping water. Ashley was looking at me like he took responsibility for it. I saw murder in his eyes.

I lifted my shirt trying to stop the blood flow. All I could think about was losing too much blood. I couldn't even hear anything anymore. When I saw the faces of them robbers, they was like ancient black statues. It was like they wasn't even real. Their faces was hard and unmoving, just like all of the black men now. They're hardened.

The leader had Ashley by the collar. I saw Marquis watching. When I could hear again dude said, "Where the shit at? You think we playin', nigga? I'll kill yo bitch ass." He put a pistol to Ashley cheek.

We ain't have no choice. I knew that was just the beginning, I could feel it. In my soul, I could feel we was on a bad road.

When they left, Ashley took his bat and threw it in the street.

Naomi came down the back steps looking concerned. Ashley punched a hole in the wall. Ashley was pissed we got robbed. Naomi grabbed my hand so I'd show her my eye.

"Still bleeding."

"Yeah."

My eye started swelling. I could feel it.

"Let me see," she said.

I could tell by her expression it was bad. I couldn't even see nothing out of it. I was seeing stars and hearing a silent hush in my ears.

They walked me to my door—Ashley, Naomi, and Marquis. It was like they was turning me over to my front door. It was like they was saying they did their part and if I was dead, at least they got me to my front door. That's how it is now, every man for himself.

When I got inside the world was getting dark. "Mama?" I couldn't even pretend I was tough no more. I started crying. I started hollering. The pain was awful. I was dizzy.

That's the last thing I remember. They said Corey and Boo got me to the hospital in an ambulance.

***

I woke, Mama was standing over me. "JuJu, what happened?"

"I don't know," I said. "He musta had some knuckles or something."

"Why was you fighting?"

"I don't know."

"You do know. Don't nobody just hit you for nothin'."

"Yes, they do."

She let out a breath.

"It's the ghetto, they'a fight you because you live next door to them. They'a fight you for anything down there. They'a just walk up to you and hit you to prove they can. It ain't like Humboldt. The people over here ain't nice like that. I told you I ain't want to move back down there. I told you it was gon' be like this. You ain't listen. I don't like it down there. I wish we ain't never move down there. I gotta fight 'em. I might have to kill 'em."

"You scaring me, boy. I didn't think I would have to worry about you like this."

"I'm sorry Mama. I don't wanna be bad. I don't want you to think I'm bad. It's just… It's just the way the streets is. You know how they say 'survival of the fittest'? It's like some niggas wanna kill you to prove they killed somebody. They wanna beat you so they can say they beat you. They wanna build a reputation off you so nobody bothers them. Ashley said we gotta get them before they get us. He right. I ain't gon' let them niggas—"

"Stop talking that 'nigga this' and 'nigga that.' You too smart for that. You ain't no dummy out in the streets. You smart. You read. You write all the time. You different."

"I'm not, Mama. I'm just a nigga."

"It ain't no such thang. Stop that. Everybody somebody. God ain't make you the way you is so you can just accept something like that. There's a purpose for you being here. For you having to live like this. That's why you read all them books. That's why you write in that notebook. I know you wanna be cool like you think them other boys is but I don't want to hear all that nigga talk from you. Them the words of a fool. I know you ain't no fool, so stop it."

Whatever Mama was saying, I ain't hear it.

***

When I was back home Ashley came to see me in my bedroom. He was different now. He was like thirty now. He looked like them dude who robbed us. His face was so hard and chiseled now. He sat on the edge of my bed.

"Yo, you straight?"

"Yeah."

"That shit hurt tho, huh?"

"Nah."

We slapped hands.

I stayed in the house for a while and recuperated. Everybody was coming to see me in my bedroom. Morris and Sean came to see me. They brought me a lot of candy, chips, and snack cakes. They was filling Mama freezer up. Mama ain't get mad because they made it about me being hurt and having to stay in the house because of what happened.

I didn't leave the house for nothin' after I almost lost my eye. Mama was real concerned. She'd come in my room and just stand there watching me. "You alright?"

"Yeah."

"Yo eye feeling better?"

"Ma, leave me alone."

I didn't wanna talk about it, I just wanted her to leave me alone. Plus, I was always watching Richard Pryor and Eddie Murphy tapes, Morris and Sean, brought over with a small TV and a VCR for my bedroom. They brought all kinds of new stuff. A cordless phone, a microwave. They even got me a new queen-size bed before I was released from the hospital. It was much bigger than the bed I had before. At first, I ain't like that it was "queen-size," cuz I ain't no girl.

Morris said, "Ain't no king bed gon' fit up them stairs."

Sean said, "We measured it. That's the biggest that'll fit."

When they brought the TV for my bedroom, Morris was telling me how I shouldn't worry about them dudes who hit me no more. Sean kept saying, "We took care of it." They wanted to tell me something about what happened, but they didn't. They just said, "They ain't gon' bother you no more. None of 'em." They was real concerned for me too. Everybody was. They kept saying I was different now.

I ain't like talking to nobody except Boo. I'd let Boo sit on the foot of my bed and watch Richard Pryor with me. She knew what it was like to be sick so she ain't ask me a lot of questions. All she'd do is just be there, so I knew she was there. She would laugh at Richard Pryor real big and I was happy she was happy. I always seen that sickle cell anemia make her cry or holler in fits of pain. She was always like that, crying, wrinkled, taking medicine. She ain't never have no peace. Even if she was in a good spot and didn't have to be hospitalized, she was still waking at night telling how she hurt so bad she couldn't sleep. I would be up with her when mama was at work and if I asked her a lot of questions, she wouldn't never be comfortable enough to get back to sleep. She would ask me to read or tell her a story. That's when I would do all my Kermit the Frog voices and make up stories about Kermit being from the ghetto. Sometimes I'd be up all night until mama came back from work.

Richard Pryor was a great storyteller. He was always taking you on a journey through life and if you listened, you'd find he wasn't telling jokes at all. He was trying to get you to understand he was just a normal man. He was trying to take away the macho bullshit black men deal with. He was saying it's okay for a black man to be vulnerable.

You don't learn that in the ghetto. In the ghetto, you have to be a robot. You have to be unemotional. At least that's what they tell you. *"Black men don't cry, for nothin'."*

One time, when I ain't laugh, Boo, turned and said, "Why you ain't laughing?"

"I am."

"No, you ain't. You want me to leave?"

"No."

It's weird, I felt better when she laughed. I just wanted to watch her be happy for once. Most people don't know what it's like to be sick. I've seen Boo in so much pain. More pain than any girl should ever be in. I've seen her just suffering for no reason. She's too nice a person to suffer like she does. She had like one hundred friends, when she ain't sick. She always asking other people how they're doing. I was just watching her laugh at Richard Pryor, and it was the best thing I ever seen.

She turned around one time and said, "You cryin?"

"No."

I didn't want her to think I ever cried. She said, "Don't be mad at them. People don't know what they be doing sometimes. I bet if that boy who hit you met you, he'd be so sorry he hit you. He'd probably beg you to forgive him. You're good, JuJu. You gon' make it out of here one day. Wait and see."

She smiled her big smile at me. I just kept trying not to cry. I wished I could be sick for both of us. I wished God would take all her pain and give it to me. Boo being sick was the worst thing I ever seen. Far worse than getting punched in the eye. I was hoping she wasn't praying for God to give all of my pain to her, but knowing her, she probably was.

32

One Sunday morning, right before August ended, Mama made me get in the car with my sisters and Corey. "You can't hide away forever in this room."

"I'm not hiding. I'm writing."

"About what?"

"This. The ghetto. Cops. Black people. All of it."

She smiled. "C'mon. Maybe we'll get a Frosty from Wendy's."

I didn't feel like I was hiding away. I just didn't feel like being out there with them. I stayed in my room so long the sun hurt my eyes when I came out with Mama and my sisters. I got in the back seat and Mama did what she always did when I'm going in the wrong direction. She took me to look at houses rich people live in.

Mama said, "You gon' live over here ain't you, JuJu?"

"Yeah, when I get rich."

Corey wasn't impressed. Mama looked at him. "What about you, babe? What kinda house you gon' buy when you grow up?" Mama smiled. My sisters laughed. I smiled.

He didn't like it. He said, "I don't think about life like that. I don't judge my life by what I got and what I ain't got. If God wanted me to have it, he'd give it to me."

It was bullshit. He was covering up his failed life by saying it didn't matter. Nothin' ever matters with people like him. Life's a big waste, or something to be taken lightly. Just exist. Just, "do what comes naturally." I didn't like people like him. I believed he still had time to make something of himself. He could still join the military or get a job digging graves, but he ain't want to. He wanted to pretend he didn't lose out on his dreams for alcohol and crack and bitterness. I told myself I would never be like him.

Mama ain't let no one live with us since Sonny lived with us a couple years ago. He was a big dude. When they first met, it was in a grocery store. We was shopping and I kept seeing him and Mama end up in the same aisle. When they finally started talking, he was laughing like crazy at my height saying, "Damn, I thought he was yo man."

"Nah that's my son. I told you to stop standing 'round me in public. People think I got a boyfriend."

Most of the time I wanted to kill Sonny. I didn't like him eating before my sisters, or talking shit to my mother. It was a long summer with Sonny, because he was telling me Mama didn't love me. When you don't know any better, you believe that shit.

Whenever he was alone with me, he'd say, "She don't like you anyway. She wish she never had you. She told me you was an ornery little motha fucka. If I don't stop her she'a put yo ass out in the street."

One time I packed a bag and left. Mama came and found me sitting on a curb. I was so mad I walked away when she pulled up with my sisters, looking at me. Mama just followed me saying, "What's wrong? What's wrong with you?"

I ain't want to talk to her about nothing. I wanted to be somewhere else. I wanted to disappear from her sight, but I couldn't. I wish I coulda been somewhere else but I ain't have nowhere to go.

That fat Sonny was always watching me. He was always telling Mama I needed a man to tell me about life. If I got mad at Mama, he'd get his fat ass involved, telling me, "A kid should stay in a kid's place."

Sometimes Mama would say, "That's my son, leave him alone." Sometimes she wouldn't say nothing. If I pissed her off too bad, she wouldn't say nothin'.

Sonny was trying to tell me all kind of man shit, but mostly he was always telling me how much I could eat.

By the time Thanksgiving came, I was so hungry I could eat all of Mama's turkey by myself. Mama kept saying she might not be able to buy Thanksgiving, but somehow, she did. We had Mama's turkey, collard greens, macaroni and cheese, mashed potatoes, sweet potato pie, and her famous cornbread stuffing. Mama, me, and my sisters and that fat Sonny ate at the table like a real family. Mama insisted. By the time we got to eat we was so hungry we ain't really say grace, Mama just said, "Thank you Lord for keeping us alive another day."

Mama was cutting us some breast meat when Sonny reached over and ripped a leg off our turkey. Mama usually used the legs and carcass for turkey soup. We'd eat her turkey for three days. Then we'd have turkey soup for two more days. Because Sonny was eating all the leg meat, I knew we wasn't gon' have Mama's turkey soup. Mama just smiled when I looked at her. I didn't say nothing because I didn't want to start problems on Thanksgiving. Sonny was eating enough for three people.

After he ate the leg meat, he turned the turkey over. "Get me some of this dark meat."

Usually I'd eat the dark meat on a sandwich, with some mayonnaise and hot sauce, but Sonny was eating it all. I couldn't stand him. I hated the way he talked. I kept thinking about punching him in the face.

Sometimes I'd wake up early the day after Thanksgiving for a turkey sandwich because I was still hungry. This time, when Sonny was staying with us, I woke up at 3:00 in the morning. Sonny was already in the kitchen, standing there in his underwear, cutting all the meat off the turkey. He was piling his stolen turkey a foot high on a slice of white bread.

I pretended I had to use the bathroom, and I just walked past him. When I was trying to pee, my stomach wouldn't stop growling. I kept thinking about knifing him in his back while he was cutting all the meat off the turkey. I smiled to myself thinking, *I should carve yo fat ass.* I left the bathroom.

On my way upstairs, he said, "You want some of this turkey?"

I was mad. "No."

Just like I thought, Mama ain't make no turkey soup. For the rest of Thanksgiving weekend, we ate a boiled egg and a bowl of oatmeal for breakfast. I wouldn't even eat dinner because we ain't have much.

Mama was making frozen hamburger all the time. She'd make three or four frozen hamburgers in the oven with onions. She'd make a pot of mashed potatoes and a can of corn. We'd have half a hamburger, a spoonful of mashed potatoes, a spoonful of corn, a piece of white bread, and some Kool-Aid for dinner. Sonny would get two hamburgers and almost half the pot of potatoes. Mama would just smile like it was fine. I couldn't never say nothing or she'd start saying I was ornery. She'd make spaghetti out of two or three frozen hamburger pucks. Sonny would say, "Because I'm a man I need more food than y'all." I thought it was bullshit. I wanted to punch him in his face, but I didn't.

We was hungry all the time. Once over a weekend, we ain't eat nothin' except fried dough. Mama kept sayin' they was "dumplings." She fooled my sisters. They was putting syrup or sugar on them "dumplings," calling them doughnuts. I compensated by stealing the school fundraising money, so I could buy a dollar's worth of lunchmeat from Webbers.

Mama and Sonny was arguing real good one day and he called Mama a bitch. I came and stood in the doorway. Mama was happy I was there, I could tell. She said, "JuJu. Go. Mind yo business." I knew she didn't mean it so I didn't move. Sonny just kept looking at me. I ain't say nothin' and he ain't say nothin'. He started looking at me real hard. He looked me up and down. He looked me from floor to ceiling. It was a ghetto fight invitation. He made a step toward me. Mama stood in front of him protecting me. I woulda fought him to the death. Mama pointed. "Go, gotdamnit." I left.

Same thing is happening again with Corey. I don't like him. I don't like living with him. I don't like him eating before my sisters. I don't like him smoking crack when Mama ain't home. He a bum. I want to throw him in the street but Mama probably take his side over mine and I'll be living with Kevin in that group home. I'd probably never see my sisters again if that happen. I'd probably finish high school with them priest Kevin live with and join the military as soon as I'm done. I'd probably never come back to Buffalo and my sisters will probably be mad at me if I did that.

I was getting used to my scar. Most people in the ghetto scared in some way, just you can't see they scar. Ashley said my scar made me look tough.

Mama didn't want me hanging with Ashley. She blamed him for my scar. I didn't. I understood if I was going to be out here, there were things that came with being out here—one of them was violence.

I was still staying in the house most of the time and Mama didn't like that either. Mostly she didn't like it because I was getting into it with Corey. Every time something came up missing, Mama blamed me. Corey was stealing money from Mama purse, so he could smoke crack. He'd always come back before Mama got off work and pretend he was home the entire day. I couldn't say nothin' or Mama would get mad at me, so I pretended like I didn't understand what was going on with him.

33

It was real crazy in the hood now. I mean real crazy. All the black boys was disappearing. All the boys was on news every morning—fifteen, sixteen, all dead or going to prison. Dozens of them. They was selling crack and shooting each other.

Living in the ghetto was like living in a warzone. Nobody's mother wanted them out after dark. Long gone was the days I hung out at Alphonso's with Ashley and Kevin. Now people were staying close to home. You see them standing on the corner or in front of their stoop, but that's it. That's as far as our mothers want us to go now. "To the corner and back. That's it." You see all the boys standing on the corner. Most of them probably had the same argument I had with Mama, with their mothers.

"Boy, don't go off this street."

"I'm not."

"I better be able to see you when I look out my door. Don't go no farther than that corner."

"Alright Mama, damn."

Most mothers like Mama now. Overprotective. Scared. Not wanting their son to be the one dead, because of crack.

This morning I just wanted to get out of the house and be like how I used to be. I got out early before the corner was full of dealers. I wanted to go to Webbers and play *Super Mario Bros* like old times.

I played *Super Mario Bros* all day and I had a better understanding of what the game was supposed to be. It was just a journey. The Everlasting board was just a test to see if you could continue through tough times. I played the Everlasting board like eight times before I figured out it was just a puzzle. You had to solve the puzzle for Mario to reach the end of his journey. There was a pattern. You'd be up, then down, then up, then down, then in the middle, before going up again—just like real life. Before long I solved the pattern and saved the princess from Bowser. I was so happy I wanted to tell Ashley about it.

When I came to his stoop he wasn't out there. He let me in. He was playing a Nintendo Entertainment System, he said he bought for a twenty. We played *Super Mario Bros* on a projection TV and sold crack through the mail slot. I kept telling him how I cleared the Everlasting board.

He said, "You can't clear it, that's why they call it the Everlasting."

"*We* call it that."

He looked at me confused. I played his Nintendo on that projection TV he bought from a crack smoker until I saved the princess again. I jumped up. "I told you. See. I told you they ain't make no game you couldn't beat. We just believed it couldn't be beat, but it could."

He was smiling. We played his NES all night and I ain't go home till past midnight. Mama was mad. She was mad at me and she was mad Corey ain't come home either.

"What yo ass doing out this late at night for?"

"We was playing the game."

"This late at night? Ain't nothin' open this late but some legs."

"I was at Ashley house."

"You ain't seen Corey out there?"

"No."

"God, I don't know what happened to my good black men but whatever it is, it ain't right. Y'all just den went crazy. Crazy. Crazy over that crack. It ain't nothin' but some gotdamn powder the white man sent for y'all stupid asses, and y'all act like this over it? Don't think I don't know you out there selling crack with that gotdamn Ashley. I told you I don't want you around that motha fucka. He gon' get yo stupid ass killed or locked up, watch."

"No, he not. I ain't selling crack."

"But Ashley is?"

"So? I ain't."

"They done already kicked yo stupid ass and almost knocked yo eye out, down there. Can't you see he ain't no good? Can't you see that? Can't you see it's you that's in trouble when you around him? Maybe you wanna die. That it? That's what you want? You mad yo father ain't come back so you wanna prove you a man?"

"No."

"Then what is it? I'd like to know."

"Nothin'. I don't know."

"G'on. Get away from me."

I went to bed.

34

Today I got dressed and came outside. When I got out, I saw a squad car in front of Ashley's house. I thought they musta busted him for selling that crack.

Ashley was being led off his stoop by police officers. It was the strangest thing I ever seen. I was just stuck there watching it like a movie. Ashley looked at me and smiled. It was the damnedest thing I ever seen. He just smiled. Like he was famous. Like he made something to be proud of out of his life.

They got in and drove off.

I stayed around there with Morris and Sean all day. They was selling crack and making money until this one redhead white dude named Woody sold Sean a stolen .45. He was talking about how he told his mother, "A nigger broke in and stole it." He was laughing his ass off. He said he had to kick in her window, so she'd believe him. "Fuck her, she'll get insurance money. I bet she won't even give me none of it. Fuckin' bitch." He kept laughing, talking about how they're looking for a "six-foot nigger, in a baseball cap." He thought that shit was funny. I ain't like it.

When I was about to leave, Woody was high as hell standing in the front window saying that the fire hydrant was his wife. I thought he was joking.

Morris and Sean was laughing. Morris said, "He trippin'."

Woody kept saying, "She following me. She following me. You see her?" He kept trying to make me look out the window. He kept saying, "She right there." He was pointing. "Look. Look. She right there." He was adamant. I looked. It was the fire hydrant.

"You see her?"

"Yeah man. I see her."

I didn't know what else to say. Part of me felt bad about it. Part of me felt sorry for him. When I was trying to talk him down Morris pushed him out the front door. Woody was frantic. He was lost. He was high on that fuckin' crack.

Morris and Sean was laughing hard.

Woody was scared, talking about his wife was gon' stab him because he "screwed her cousin." He was banging on the door trying to get in. Sean kept saying, "Man she close. She got the knife. She on yo ass. Watch out. Oh shit. Run."

When they opened the door Woody ran past us, into the basement. Morris and Sean ain't never laugh so hard.

"She gon' kill me. She gon' kill me."

I heard him talking to himself.

"Baby I'm sorry. Tell her I'm sorry. Baby I'm sorry." That crack was screwing up everybody.

***

Ashley ain't come home and he wasn't in the police station. Naomi was calling every police station in Buffalo, looking for him, but no one had him. Naomi was lost, talking in circles. We waited for hours. Naomi kept saying she hoped they didn't kill him. "This ain't right. Something ain't right."

When it was almost dark, a police car parked in front of their house. I was still on the stoop. Me and Marquis. They got Ashley out the trunk. He was all sweaty and thirsty looking. Ashely could barely stand. They held him for a minute then they let him go. Ashley walked past us with his head down.

Naomi asked, "You alright?"

He didn't answer.

Naomi said, "What did you do to him, you bastards." The cops just laughed their faces off.

Ashley came out with a shoe box and gave it to them. They left. They even blew the horn as they pulled away from the curb. I guess they must have thought it was funny to put Ashley in the trunk and rob him of his drug money.

Naomi looked like Ashley's mother with her concerned face. "What happened?"

"Nothin'."

"Somethin'. Ashley, tell me. We need to do somethin'."

"We can't do nothin'."

"Well, what did they want?"

"You know what they wanted. Money. They wanted money. I said I ain't givin' them nothin' and they put me in the trunk."

"And that's it?"

"They drove me around for like an hour hitting bumps, laughing. Then they opened the trunk and asked if I was gon' give them something. I said no, and they closed the trunk. Next time they opened the trunk I said no again, and they got me out the trunk and put me in the backseat. I thought they was taking me to jail but they didn't. They took me over there off Johnson and pulled up on some dudes out there. They started patting them down asking me, 'Is he the one?' They was trying to make it so people would think I'm a snitch. They was trying to make them think I brought the cops over there. I told them I ain't have nothin' so they put me back in the trunk. They opened it one last time talking about I might get reported missing and all that, trying to scare me. I told them I ain't no bitch. They said they was gon' arrest you and put Marquis in a foster home."

Ashley ain't sell no crack that night. We played *Super Mario Bros* for a while. He looked lost. He looked *'shamed.* That's what Mama always said when my face was wrong. "Don't be 'shamed. What shamed you, boy? People want you 'shamed so they can take advantage of you."

Ashley said. "You still write?"

"Little bit."

"I'm telling you man, people want you to fail. Even people you think love you. Even yo mama. They scared. They don't think we can make it. I don't give a fuck what they think no more. I'm gon' be the best I can be. I was born for this shit. They don't understand that. They think they like me. They ain't like me. I ain't never goin' back to being hungry. Never. This shit don't mean nothin' to me. Life, death—fuck that. I ain't gon' let them take shit from me. They'a do anything ta keep you at the bottom. Ta keep you from being yo best. They wanna be better than you. They wanna say they better than you. I don't accept that. They ain't gon' do that shit to me. I ain't gon' get in line. I ain't waiting my turn. Fuck that."

Ashley wasn't normal after what them cops did to him. He was on a mission. He said he was the best crack dealer in Buffalo, and he was gon' "take over Buffalo, one day." By the end of the week he was selling crack and shooting black boys. Naomi couldn't tell him nothin', neither could anyone else. He was all proud now, walking around with his chest out talking about can't nobody do nothin' to him, "not even the police." It was like he believed he wouldn't never be arrested after them crooked cops didn't arrest him. He wasn't scared of nothin' no more, not even death.

One time he went right to a crack house and told them they had to close down, or he was gon' kill everybody in it. I couldn't stop him. He said, "Don't be no sucka, JuJu. All you gotta do is just stand there." He gave me a ski mask. He gave me a pistol. I ain't do it. Nothin' I said worked. He was mad. He did it by himself. I told him there are some things we can't come back from. Like death.

"You be scared with yo tail tucked between yo legs," he sneered.

This morning he was out front of a crack house with a rifle in a garbage bag; they thought he was joking till he shot right through their door. Naomi was real scared. She kept asking me to "talk to him." I couldn't tell him nothin'. When Naomi seen how bad he was, she thought somebody might kill him.

He said, "They ain't gon' kill me 'cus I'ma kill them first."

Naomi just cried for a minute. She ain't say nothing, she just looked at my face and cried. It felt like she was his mother. I shrugged. There was nothing I could say to him.

She said, "Oh God. Oh God, what did you do to my black men? God, why is it like this? This boy talkin' 'bout he gon' kill people. Oh God, please help him. Please, God, help him see this ain't no way to be. Please Lord." She begged him to stop selling crack.

Ashley laughed the biggest laugh I ever seen on him. "Stop? You crazy? All this money I'm makin'."

"Money ain't worth yo life, fool."

"What life? What life I got without money? What life any black man got in America, without money?"

"What life you got if they kill you, fool?"

Ashley smiled. He wasn't buying it.

"Please, Ashley. We don't need this kind of money where you have to shoot people. Just stop. We doing alright. You can finish school. You said you wanted to deliver the mail once. You can still do that. You can have a good life and be a good man."

"Ain't no good life. Only chance I got to be my own man is in the streets. White people don't want me having no good life. They built it so a black man gotta struggle. I can't wake up one day and get no factory job making $40,000 like a white boy could. A white boy could get drunk till he twenty-five and go and work in a coal mine making $70,000. You think they gon' let us have that kind of choice? No. They want us to be hungry. They want us to be beggin'. They want us to work for three dollars. That ain't gon' be me. I'ma be rich. And if they kill me everybody gon' see on the news I was out here making it for myself. I ain't beg no white man one time for his benevolence. Fuck that.

"That's how they want us anyway," he went on, "beggin'. That's what they want. They want it so we gotta depend on they charity. They want to feel high and mighty after all that shit, they do. After they come around here bussin' our heads open. They think God gon' use they charity as a way to forgive them for what they've done. For how they keep us packed up in this ghetto and going in and out of jail because they keep all the good shit for themselves. Don't never take they charity. Fuck 'em. Don't make them feel better about the shit they be doing to us. I'd rather die in jail, than make them feel good. I'd rather die in these streets. Fuck you. Stick yo charity up yo ass."

"Ashley, you're smarter than this. Didn't you want to be a lawyer?"

"No, Gran'ma wanted me to be a lawyer."

Suddenly it seemed that all the guns in the ghetto started shooting Ashley's house. Ashley was shooting back. Naomi and Marquis dropped to the floor. A bullet came right through the wall and went up in the ceiling—it scared the hell out of me. Another inch and it woulda went through my skull. I got down, I got down fast. I was holding my head and they just kept shooting.

When it was over, a hundred police cars was in front of Ashley's house. They took Ashley out in cuffs. He was just smiling like he was famous. They took his guns but they ain't find the drugs he buried in his bedroom wall.

The police came door to door asking who saw the drive by. That old lady who lived on the side of us, opposite from Ashley, said, "You let me live in yo house, you live here, and I'a tell you all you need to know." Ain't nobody tell nothin'.

A lot of black boys act like Ashley now. They ain't scared of nothin', not even Morris. All the black boys selling crack and trying to get the rest of us to sell crack with them, or for them. They all black boys who dropped out of high school like Morris and Sean and Ashley and Tone and Henry and a hundred other black boys I ain't know. They was all saying the same thing to boys like me, to get us to fall in line. Trying to make it so we couldn't think for ourselves. When Ashley said he was dropping out of school, he got mad because I said I was going to school in September. He kept trying to make it so I'd choose crack and crack money, over school.

"Man, school ain't gon' get you nothin'. What you gon' do, get a job for a white man?"

"No I'ma get a job for myself."

"You gon' still be working for the white man."

"No, I ain't. I'ma be working for myself. If I make a paycheck it go in my pocket, not a white man's."

"But the white man gon' make more than you."

I hated that way of thinking. A lot of people in the ghetto think if you trying to get somewhere, you doing it for the white man. That's how they keep a lot of black boys locked in the trap. Either you gotta work for the white man or sell drugs or turn up pimping or shooting and that's all you can do. I hated it. I didn't want my mind to think like that. I wanted to think I was working hard for myself, if I had a job.

Ashley would pull a wad of cash out of his pocket, to convince me. "Get money. Live while we young. Fuck them white people. They gon' keep telling you to wait yo turn. Fuck that. I wanna live good, right now."

I thought so hard about selling crack with him, but I didn't. I couldn't. I thought it was stupid. They was trying to make it like they was special or something. They was saying, "Man, let's get this money." Then they'd show you a bunch of cash from their pocket. But really what they was doing was, they was trying to make it so we had to look up to them. They wanted us to envy all that money they was making. They was trying to act like they was famous and we wasn't.

One day Henry pulled up on me in a nice black BMW. "Yo, JuJu, let me talk to you for a minute."

I stood at the passenger side.

"Yo. I'm sayin'. 'Member we was selling them raffle tickets? We was getting money, right?"

"Word."

He gave me some dap. "Get in. I wanna talk to you."

We rode around for a minute. "We can get this money. See, you smart. Like me. I'm sayin' we ain't like them. We ain't never have no problems with them tickets. We got money. You got yo cut. I got my cut. It's nothin'." He was telling me how he could give me some crack and I could sell it and we could split the money. I turned him down. When I got out, he said, "Think about it."

I was always telling them I was gon' think about it, but I had already decided I wasn't gon' be nobody's flunky. Plus, I thought it was stupid to sell crack to my own people and watch them walk around like they was dead. It just didn't sit right with me.

Even Tone tried to get me on his side. One day when I was going to Webbers, Tone was standing out there with his boys. "JuJu." He said, "JuJu? Yo, I'm talkin' to you." He said, "Yo. Didn't you used to play corner?"

"Yeah. For a minute."

I did too, but I got sick and had to quit. They had to take out my appendix. I was sick real bad, but not as sick as Boo. Mama was scared. She kept saying, "What if somebody hit you out there and split yo stomach wide open?" So, I ain't play football no more.

Tone looked me over. "You wanna make some money?"

In the ghetto you have to hear them out, or they start talking that "You disrespecting me" bullshit. I just looked at him.

He pointed. "See that bag right there?"

It was a Doritos bag.

"Yeah."

"Jake run up, you snatch that shit and run. Hit the shortcuts and shit."

I laughed. "Get outta here wit that bullshit. You think I'm a fool?"

Jake is slang for a white police officer. In the ghetto, police officers chase the runner. This dude think I'ma run and get caught so he can stroll off the block. He must think I'm stupid.

"Yo, JuJu, I'a give you a hun'dred dollas."

I walked away.

"Yo? Here. You don't want this money? Pussy nigga. JuJu, you a bitch."

I kept walking. It wasn't worth it. Not even for the sake of my reputation. Plus, it's different now. Reputations lead to killings. I was seeing it different. I wanted to be low-key. I wanted to fade into the background. I didn't want to be out there risking being shot over nothin'.

These dealers, they all the same. They all looking for a fool to pull the trigger for them, so they can walk away clean. They getting a lot of boys on they side like that. They offering them money and drugs and girls and all kinds of shit boys in the ghetto ain't never have. It's like I told Ashley, when he kept saying, "All you gotta do is go dumb on these niggas."

"If I do some dumb shit, I'm doing it for myself."

Thing is, if you don't pick a side. If you ain't with them. They don't like you. "You either with me or you against me."

35

I was going to Webbers for some junk food for me and my sisters. When I got out there, Tone and his boys was standing out there. They was selling crack.

Tone's boy said, "You smokin'?"

"Nah, man."

They laughed.

"You hustlin'?"

"Nah."

"You lying to me?"

Tone said, "That's Ashley homeboy. Morris little brother."

"I'on give a fuck. You hustlin'?"

I ain't say nothin'.

Tone said, "You know they got his boy locked up."

Tone's boy said, "You holding?"

"Psshhht. Nah man."

"You ain't holding for Ashley?"

"Fuck no."

I tried to enter Webbers, but Tone's boy grabbed me by the shirt. I looked him in his eye. He put a pistol on my heart.

"You lyin' to me?"

"No."

My heart was beating worse than when that cop tried to get me locked up over them sneakers Ashley and Kevin stole.

"What'chu got in yo pockets?"

"Nothin'. I got a dollar."

He reached inside my pocket and took the five-dollar bill I had. Morris said, *"Never keep more than five dollars on you because a crackhead will kill you for twenty."*

"Thought you only had a dollar, bitch."

"That's my sisters' money."

"Nigga, that's mine." He put it in his pocket. I was reaching for it. He put his gun right in my face. "Get yo bitch ass outta here."

Tone said, "Should shoot yo bitch ass for all that shit yo man be talkin'."

Tone's boy said, "And get Morris, fuck that nigga. He bleed too."

I looked him in his eye. I wanted to fight him so bad. I couldn't do nothin'. He had his gun right in my face. They all had guns, I could tell.

I went home.

Mama said, "What's the matter?"

"They robbed me."

I was mad. I was looking for something. A knife. A hammer. Something. I still had that pistol Ashley gave me under my mattress. I ran up to get it. When I tried to leave, Mama stood in front of the door.

"I can't let you out there."

I was mad. "What?"

Man, I was mad. I could kill them. I could kill them all. I wanted to walk up to them and just start shooting. I could see it in my mind. Just shoot them and run home. I ain't even want to talk to them or nothin'. I had it all planned out in my mind. Kill them. Run home. Make Mama drive me to Alabama to live with Aunt Francis. She got a big farm the family bought a little at a time while they was sharecropping for the white man. Francis and my great uncles worked and bought land. That's all they did. They said they wanted to own all the land my great-grandfather was a slave on. They owned most of it too.

Mama was blocking the door.

"Move."

"No."

"Move, Mama."

"You gon' push me too?"

"I ain't trying to push you. Move."

"I can't let you do what you think you need to do. You fine. You home. Let it go."

"No. Bump that. And he put a gun in my face. Bump that."

"JuJu, I can't let you go outside no more."

"What?"

Boo came behind me. "It's just junk food, we don't need it anyway. I don't want you to die, JuJu." She hugged me real tight. I lost a tear. "Don't let it get to you."

"What I'm supposed to do—hide? I can't never live no more."

Mama said, "They is crazy for that crack. I don't wanna have no funeral for my child. You hear me?" Mama had a tear. "I know you want revenge for that scar on yo eye. That ain't gon' do nothin' but get you killed. They killin' over that crack. They just killing each other dead out there. They don't care no more. They'a kill anybody now. Promise me you ain't gon' do nothing stupid."

I was mad. I wanted to get revenge.

"Promise me, JuJu."

Boo said, "Who gon' read with me if they kill you?"

All of my sisters was saying they loved me and I ain't have to prove I was tough by killing. Mama called Morris. He came over looking mean. Him and Sean. They wanted me to tell them all about it.

***

That night I was in my bedroom reading *The Catcher in the Rye*, listening to them outside shooting each other. I could hear them shooting all night. *The Catcher in the Rye* was cool, because even though Holden had everything a kid could want, he still had problems. With all the sirens outside I couldn't concentrate on reading. It got so bad I put on my Walkman, so I couldn't hear it.

In the morning, I saw on the news that somebody killed Antonio Lamar Davis, in a drive-by shooting. That's Tone's real name.

Every night was the same after that. Shootings. Sirens. Dead black boys. Black boys being led off in handcuffs. I couldn't even sleep most of the time. I was always dreaming they was gon' shoot me and I'd wake up sweaty. Sometimes I'd dream I was the shooter and I'd wake just before I shot them.

I was scared to sleep, so I'd stay up writing, reading, or listening to music.

36

I still got more story with Morris and Sean and Ashley, but that ain't why I wrote this book. I could tell you how Chill got fifteen years in the penitentiary, or how them Fruit Belt Boys killed Dondon and left Ronron, holding him while his blood ran out. I could tell you how they got Ronron a couple weeks later when he tried to get revenge. I could tell you how Sean is doing thirty-five years in the federal penitentiary. I could tell you how Kevin is strung out on crack, doing home invasions and robbing drug dealers. I could tell you how dealers keep trying to show you money they can't never spend on nothing except clothes, furniture, used cars, and funerals. That's how Morris was. He had a million twenties stacked up in that bedroom in Mama house. He kept talking about what he was gon' do with the money.

In the end he ain't do nothin' with it. He got paralyzed in a drive-by shooting and the government took all his crack money to buy new police cars, so they could look good in new cars when they bust future drug dealers.

I could even tell you about how they killed Ashley one night while I was in bed listening to my Walkman. I could tell you how nobody came to Ashley's funeral except me, Naomi, Mama, and Marquis. Even Ashley's mother didn't come to his funeral.

I could tell you about how Broadway is really bad now and how women walk the street almost naked trying to sell themselves, even when it's snowing. I could tell you how Ashley's mother grabbed my arm one time and said she'd have sex with me for a twenty.

I could tell you all of that, but I know don't nobody care about that. Don't nobody care about little black boys from the ghetto. So, I want to tell you about what happened to Boo.

I hadn't noticed it before she died but Boo was my best friend. When she died, it was like part of me died too. Reading and talking about all them books with her at the time seemed like a chore. Seemed like something I did for her. When she was gone, I knew it was the other way around. I knew she was doing it for me.

Most of the time she was barely able to go to school. She'd spend nearly half her days in the hospital getting blood transfusions, going from regular floors to ICU. Even through all that she'd still lay there sick, writhing in pain asking about me. She'd ask about my writing every time I visited.

Right before school started, she was in the hospital in a ball of agony. When she saw I was standing there looking at her she smiled though her pain.

"You alright?" I asked.

"Yeah," she mumbled.

She had one of them pain pump buttons in her hand. I saw she squeezed it.

"How's your writing?" she muttered. Right before her medicine put her to sleep.

When she was back home, I finished *Catcher in the Rye*. Mama had to bring dinner to her bedroom. I was in there with her talking about the book. She'd always steer our conversation back to my writing and the book I want to write.

"It's about being from the ghetto."

"But how does it end? Your book, it needs an ending. It needs to be about something."

"What'd you mean?"

She was always confusing me. She was smarter than me. She even won an essay contest at the Montessori school one time.

"You can't write an entire book about living in the ghetto. It has to be about something. Like, *Catcher in the Rye* ain't about skippin' school or flunkin' out. It's about teenaged alienation. Your book has to be about something. Something you believe in."

That was our last conversation before she died.

When we was walking to the bus stop one morning she just stopped.

"You alright?" I asked.

She just looked different. Her eyes. Her face. She was just different.

"Boo?" I said.

"I wanna go home," she replied.

We didn't go to school that day. It just seemed wrong. It was like someone whispered something in her ear.

She just lost her strength all at once. She just looked at me and fell onto me. I got her home. She had her arm wrapped around my shoulder.

She said, "JuJu, I feel like I'ma die."

"No, you not. Don't say that."

"I am, JuJu. Tell Mama I'm sorry."

I don't never really cry. Anyway, I try not to.

When I got her to the door she said, "You should read L*ord of the Flies*."

"What?"

"It's a good book. You gon' like it, I swear."

That was the last thing she ever said to me. Sometimes at night I hear her say, "You gon' like it, I swear."

Soon as we got in the house she fell on the couch. She was twisting and turning into a ball of agony.

Corey came out of Mama's room. "What happened?"

I wanted to say, *Nothin'. It ain't none of yo business. Go smoke yo crack.* But I didn't. "She sick."

"You call yo mama?"

"No."

Boo just screamed real bad. She had this look in her eye like she was gon' die. Then she stopped screaming. She was breathing real bad. Panting.

"Call yo mama." Corey gave me the phone. I called 911.

***

When we was in the hospital Mama was crying real bad. They made her fill out some papers about Boo's life. Mama ain't hardly write nothing because she was crying on the papers, they gave us. Her handwriting was shaky, so I wrote it for her. It was like a contact the hospital used to protect itself. When the nurse was talking about that contract all I heard was, "If she die, it ain't our fault, okay?" That last "okay?" was said with fake concern from the nurse. "We're gonna try and do this. We're gonna try and do that. It might not work, okay?"

When Boo was dead, I was standing in Children's Hospital, looking out the window. They had just gave out one of them code blues. I knew it was Boo. I could feel it. I was hoping it wasn't but I knew it was her.

I had this thought during Boo's funeral. I wrote it down. *When everything is dying, you think about life.* That's what happened to me.

I never saw life the same. I never saw myself the same. I never saw anything the same. I was thinking about life. I was thinking about escaping my life.

Mama was only happy one time since Boo's death. She came home from work one time, saying she got a new job at Buffalo General Hospital. She said she gon' be "making more with one job than I did with three." She said she was gon' buy a house and we was gon' move off Guilford, "before it get too late." Before I end up like Morris and Sean, or Ashley. She was real worried about me.

I stayed up all night writing and reading, thinking about the books I read with Boo. I was thinking about *To Kill a Mockingbird.* Boo said the title is saying, "It's okay to kill a black man, but not okay to kill a bird." It was the only book I could talk about like that. Like in an interpretation.

"But it's more than that," I said. "Harper Lee was saying white people are hypocrites about race. It wasn't just killing a black man, it's also we're all the same kind of judgmental A-hole, looking to elevate ourselves higher, socially."

I was thinking about the Ewells. Them Ewells was treated like scum and if they found something, some love or something, outside what society said was right, it broke the hierarchy. Them Ewells ain't supposed to be happy. Them Ewells supposed to be shit and understand they shit. They ain't supposed to never challenge for a better life, or love, or nothin'. *Them*

Ewells is like black people in the ghetto. We supposed to know we ain't shit. We supposed to know we can't never be as good as white people.

Thing is, a lot of black people believe it, just as much as white people. In the ghetto they circle your mind into believing you have to do ghetto things. They tell you, "We from the ghetto, this what we do." If you say, "Not me, I'ma be a writer," they get mad and laugh. They say, "The white man ain't gon' let you." I don't think like that. I think about being free. I think about being the best me I can be. I just want to have freedom. Freedom from society and ghetto rules and restrictions. I want to be free to think. To think for myself. To be my own man. To go my own way.

***

When I got into high school, I didn't have to go to Kensington or South Park because Mama bought a little house with the insurance money she got for Boo. It was the best place we ever lived in. The street was quiet, like Humboldt Parkway. The entire street was black homeowners. I had this English teacher, Mrs. Baldwin. She was telling us how everything in the ghetto can be washed away through education.

"Can't nobody stop you from becoming a doctor. Or a lawyer. Or a teacher. Or an engineer. We can control our future," she said.

That was her big saying. "We control our future."

On our first week she made us write one of them papers about our summer. I told how Boo died from Sickle Cell Anemia.

When she was handing papers back, she smiled at me.

"You're not supposed to make me cry, JuJu. Didn't you have any fun?"

I raised my eyebrows because I didn't know what to say.

As the year progressed, Mrs. Baldwin got to know me for my papers. She'd give back papers with a red smile on them. Words would say *Good job* and *Well done.*

She assigned *Black Boy* by Richard Wright, *An American Slave* by Frederick Douglass, as well as extra credit for reading, *The Autobiography of Malcolm X.*

With Mrs. Baldwin's help I started to see the ghetto is the deepest underbelly of survival and poverty. A construct of classism being supported through racism. I was determined to write my own book about overcoming poverty and blackness. I asked Mrs. Baldwin about becoming a writer.

"Who gon' stop you?" she said. "We control our future."

Tamario Pettigrew was born on July 16, 1973, in Buffalo, New York, and he still resides there today. He's a graduate of The University at Buffalo, where he earned a BA in History and attended the MA program. He began writing short stories in 2014 while an inpatient at Buffalo General Hospital, where he was being treated for, Sickle Cell Anemia.

DEC 2019

CPSIA information can be obtained
at www.ICGtesting.com
Printed in the USA
LVHW091754041219
639425LV00002B/326/P